P9-ART-945

# STEEL BATTERING STEEL

With the train racing along the track toward the oncoming headlight, Jim climbed down the cab's steps and hung on. He looked at the ground rushing beneath him, moving so fast that it was a blur. Then, steeling himself, he took a deep breath and pushed himself away from the engine, leaping as far as he could. He hit the ground with a bone-jarring thud, then tumbled and bounced painfully for several yards. Finally, he rolled to a stop. Although every part of his body ached, he was sure nothing was broken. Pulling himself to his feet, he watched, his heart pounding, as the two engines raced toward each other. . . .

*Berkley Boulevard titles by Robert Vaughan*

THE WILD WILD WEST
THE WILD WILD WEST: THE NIGHT OF THE DEATH TRAIN
THE WILD WILD WEST: THE NIGHT OF THE ASSASSIN

# THE WILD WILD WEST™

## THE NIGHT OF THE ASSASSIN

## ROBERT VAUGHAN

BERKLEY BOULEVARD BOOKS, NEW YORK

If you purchased this book without a cover, you should be aware that this book is stolen property. It was reported as "unsold and destroyed" to the publisher, and neither the author nor the publisher has received any payment for this "stripped book."

THE WILD WILD WEST: THE NIGHT OF THE ASSASSIN

A Berkley Boulevard Book / published by arrangement with
Viacom Consumer Products, Inc.

PRINTING HISTORY
Berkley Boulevard edition / December 1998

All rights reserved.
Copyright © 1998 by CBS, Inc.
Cover design by Steven Ferlauto.
This book may not be reproduced in whole or in part,
by mimeograph or any other means, without permission.
For information address: The Berkley Publishing Group,
a member of Penguin Putnam Inc.,
375 Hudson Street, New York, New York 10014.

The Penguin Putnam Inc. World Wide Web site address is
http://www.penguinputnam.com

ISBN: 0-425-16517-5

BERKLEY BOULEVARD
Berkley Boulevard Books are published by The Berkley Publishing Group,
a member of Penguin Putnam Inc.,
375 Hudson Street, New York, New York 10014.
BERKLEY BOULEVARD and its logo
are trademarks belonging to Berkley Publishing Corporation.

PRINTED IN THE UNITED STATES OF AMERICA

10  9  8  7  6  5  4  3  2  1

# THE WILD WILD WEST™

## THE NIGHT OF THE ASSASSIN

# 1

*Washington, D.C.*
*April 14, 1865*

As the train from Virginia crossed the Potomac River early on the morning of April 14, Captain James T. West of the United States Army looked through the window at the city of Washington. A long layer of haze lay over the city, filtering the sun and turning it into a fiery red disk as it rose on the eastern horizon. The smoke from twenty thousand fires—breakfast stoves, fireplaces, and heating furnaces, all lit to push back the chill—formed the haze. With spring not yet a month old, the nights and early mornings were still cold.

Jim stretched his legs out in front of him. They were stiff and cramped after the long ride from Richmond. He had dozed fitfully during the night and would be glad when the train finally pulled into the depot. The air in the car was close, acrid with smoke from the wood burning in its heating stove, and coal oil from the lamps. It was also heavy with the smell of too many people packed too closely together.

The front door to the car opened, and the conductor came

through. "Washin'ton," he called. "We'll be pullin' into the station in five minutes. This is Washin'ton."

When the train stopped a few minutes later, Jim disembarked with the other passengers. Pausing briefly on the platform, he pulled his uniform cape around him against the chill, then collected his bag and walked out to catch one of the horsecars.

Until a few days ago, Jim had been an intelligence officer on General Grant's staff. In General Grant's last dispatch from Appomatox, he mentioned Captain West as having "contributed significantly to the success of our army through his intelligence-gathering efforts." Now he was in Washington to be discharged from the service and start life as a civilian.

A cab pulled up beside him and stopped. The driver set his brake, then looked down at Jim.

"Well, me boyo, 'tis welcome to Washington you are," the hack driver said. "And lucky for you I came along when I did, for anyone will tell you, Paddy O'Brien is the finest hack driver in all the city." The driver was wearing an old military greatcoat, devoid of any insignia. He was also wearing a kelly green top hat, chin whiskers, and a pair of wire-rim glasses. The stump of a pipe was clamped in his teeth.

"Thank you, but I plan to take the horsecar," Jim replied.

"Nonsense . . . the horsecars go only where the track takes them. You tell Paddy where you want to go, and I can take you right to the front door," the driver said. Before Jim could protest, the driver had already hopped down and tossed the luggage into the cab. With an ingratiating smile, he held out his hand in invitation. "At your service, sir."

Jim shook his head, then chuckled. "All right, you win."

Jim climbed into the hack, then leaned back in the well-cushioned leather seat to look out over the city. What he saw both shocked and surprised him.

Washington had undergone a considerable change since the last time Jim had seen it. During the war, it had grown into a sprawling city of seventy-five thousand people, but the growth had been sudden and unplanned. What he stared at now was a strange jumble of muddy, unpaved streets riddled with potholes and lined with simple low frame or brick houses. The scene was jarring because these little structures were dominated by half a dozen magnificent marble buildings built in the classical Greek style.

A canal ran through the middle of the city. Originally used for small boat traffic, it was now a sluggish, pestilence-breeding waterway. It was the receptacle of all the city's sewers, and no one could cross the bridges that spanned it without holding their breath against the foul odors.

"We'll be away from the stench in a couple of minutes," the driver said when he saw Jim's reaction.

"How do the people stand it?" Jim asked.

"You can get used to almost anything," the driver replied. "Sure, 'n you would be knowin' that, boyo, considering where you've been."

Jim thought of the battlefields, where he had seen thousands of men wounded and dying.

"Yes," he said. "I do know that."

It was a drive of fifteen minutes from the depot to the United States Treasury Building. There, after paying the cab fare, Jim found his way to the anteroom just outside the office of the secretary of treasury, Hugh McCulloch. McCulloch had very recently replaced Salmon Chase as secretary of treasury in President Lincoln's cabinet.

Jim walked up to the clerk. "I'm . . ."

"Captain West?" the clerk responded before Jim could finish introducing himself. "Yes, you may go in, sir. The secretary is expecting you."

"Thank you."

Secretary McCulloch greeted Jim when he stepped into the office. "Thank you for coming, Captain West."

"A personal invitation from a cabinet officer is not something you take lightly," Jim said. "Though I must say, I don't know why the secretary of the treasury would want to see me. I'm not an economist."

McCulloch laughed. "Not an economist," he repeated. "That's good. Have a seat, Captain."

Jim sat down, then accepted the secretary's offer of a cigar.

"Captain West, how do you feel about paper money?"

"Paper money? I don't particularly like it, sir."

"Why not?"

"Not everyone is willing to accept it. They want gold or silver coins."

McCulloch nodded. "That's true. But we are now a nation of many millions of people . . . a reunited nation, I should say. And we have an economy that is measured, not in the millions, but in the billions of dollars. Paper currency is the most efficient means of maintaining an economic system this large, but until our citizens can trust the money, this will never come about. And who can blame them for not trusting paper currency? Nearly one-third of all paper money now in circulation is counterfeit, and the situation is getting worse. I'm sure you can see the potential for disaster."

"Yes, sir, that could be a problem," Jim replied, still not certain what was expected of him.

"President Lincoln has authorized the formation of a Secret Service, to fall under the auspices of the United States Treasury Department. The purpose of the Secret Service would be to search out, find, and arrest, by whatever means possible, those who produce and circulate counterfeit money. The Secret Service will have law-enforcement jurisdiction that supercedes all local, county, state, or territorial law-enforcement agencies."

"You mean like a federal police force?"

"Yes, with far-reaching authority. A successful agent would be one who is resourceful, daring, and dedicated. In other words, the qualities that one needs to be a good intelligence officer. And, according to General Grant, you were one of the best. So, the question I have now is, would you be interested in such a job?"

"Yes," Jim replied. "Yes, I think I would be."

"Good. Now, we have decided that our agents should

all be dispatched in two-man teams, so I would like you to meet your new partner."

McCulloch went to a side door, opened it, and said something to someone standing just outside. The man who came in was about the same size and age as Jim.

"This is Artemus Gordon," McCulloch said. "Mr. Gordon, this is Captain . . . though I take it, soon to be Mister . . . James T. West."

Jim and Artemus shook hands, then Jim got a puzzled look on his face and stared, hard, at Artemus.

"Have we met, Mr. Gordon?"

Artemus laughed. "Very good, Mr. West. You'll make a fine agent." Then, in a thick Irish brogue, he said, "Well, me boyo, 'tis welcome to Washington you are. And lucky for you I came along when I did, for anyone will tell you, I'm the finest hack driver in all the city."

"You're Paddy O'Brien!" Jim said, in surprise.

"No, but I am the man who posed as Paddy O'Brien."

"Well, you were very good at it. You certainly had me fooled." Jim got a confused look on his face. "But I am curious as to why you wanted to."

"Secretary McCulloch told me what train you would be arriving on. I knew all about you from the reports General Grant filed, but I knew you didn't know anything about me. I guess you might say I was auditioning for you."

Jim chuckled. "In that case, you passed your audition."

"Mr. West, I think the two of you will make a very good team," McCulloch said, "with your experience in the field of intelligence work, and Mr. Gordon's acting experience."

"Acting?" Jim said, looking at Artemus. "You are an actor?"

"Alas, that is true," Artemus said. "I am but a poor player who struts and frets his brief hour upon the stage."

"And, as you can tell from having been fooled by him, Mr. West, he is also a master of disguise," McCulloch pointed out. "From time to time that may be a talent you would find useful."

"I'm sure it will be useful," Jim replied.

"Now, how soon would you like to start?"

"My discharge does not take effect until midnight tonight. I can start tomorrow, if you'd like," said Jim.

"Great. In the meantime, why don't you take in a few of the sights of our capitol city? In fact, here is something you might find amusing. I believe President Lincoln is attending a play tonight at Ford Theater. It just so happens that I have two tickets that I won't be using. They are yours, if you want them."

McCulloch held out the tickets and Artemus took them from him. He looked at them. "*Our American Cousin,*" he read.

"Do you know the play?" McCulloch asked.

"Yes. It's pretty worn-out, but it does have a few good laugh lines."

"Well, I am not a drama critic, Mr. Gordon, but I could use a few laughs," Jim said,

"Then laugh we shall, Captain West," Artemus replied.

"I've also taken rooms for the two of you over at the National Hotel," McCulloch said. "Oh, and eat heartily, gentlemen, the meals are courtesy of the Treasury Department."

"I could get used to all this very quickly," Artemus said.

The National Hotel was a massive red-brick building, so large that it occupied an entire block on Sixth Avenue between Pennsylvania and C Streets. As Jim and Artemus registered for their rooms, a strikingly handsome young man, dressed in riding clothes, strode through the lobby. The clerk spotted him, then leaned across the counter. "Do you see that gentleman?" he whispered as he pointed the man out to Jim and Artemus. "That is John Wilkes Booth, a very famous actor. Would you like to meet him? I could call him over and introduce you to him, if you would like."

Before Jim or Artemus could answer, the clerk called to Booth. The dark-haired man smiled and headed toward the counter.

"Mr. Booth!" the clerk exclaimed, relishing the opportunity to introduce a famous actor. "This is Artemus Gordon and Captain James West. Captain West is on General Grant's staff.''

''I was on his staff,'' Jim corrected. ''As of midnight tonight, I will be a civilian.''

''Nevertheless, he is one of the real heroes of this war,'' the clerk said.

''I wouldn't say hero,'' Jim replied, growing increasingly uncomfortable with the clerk's need to embellish what little he knew.

Booth eyed Jim and brushed his thick dark mustache with a gloved finger. ''Yes, hero or villain, I suppose it would all depend upon which side one's sympathies were with, wouldn't it?''

Jim thought it was a rather strange thing to say, but Booth then tempered the remark with a broad smile.

''Perhaps I shall get to see some of your heroics tonight,'' Jim suggested. ''I'll be attending *Our American Cousin.*''

''No, Mr. Booth won't be in that play,'' Artemus said. ''He is more of a classical actor.''

Booth looked more closely at Artemus. ''I have a feeling that I know you, sir.''

''Like you, Mr. Booth, I am an actor. Though with only modest success.''

Booth laughed. ''Perhaps that is your problem, sir. Modesty does not become the actor.'' Booth started to leave, then he turned, and holding up a finger, waved it dramatically. ''I may not be in the play, but I do believe you will see a particularly fine performance tonight.'' He touched the brim of his riding cap and continued on his way.

''Artie, are all actors that odd?''

''Absolutely, Jim,'' Artemus replied. ''Of the entire breed, only I am normal.''

Jim laughed.

At curtain time, President Lincoln had not yet arrived at the theater, but the actors, not waiting for him to appear, began the production. Despite President Lincoln's absence, the audience was enjoying the performance. It was a comedy, and the actors were portraying wildly caricatured figures. In addition, the mood of the theatergoers, celebrating the end of the war, was so jubilant that lines that would not have received a chuckle two months earlier were now being greeted with uproarious laughter.

As Artemus had remarked, the play was a little worn. Laura Keene and her theater company had been presenting *Our American Cousin* since 1858. Many of the actors had more than one role, and the actor who played the male comic lead, Harry Hawk, was also Laura Keene's business manager.

The attractive, gracious British actress had won the hearts of her cast and audiences alike and had already performed the leading role of Florence Trenchard, which had been created just for her, more than one thousand times over during the last seven years.

But none of that seemed to matter to the audience. The joyful mood of the city, the intimacy of being in the theater, and the fact that so many of the sixteen hundred people in the audience had seen the play before, all contributed to making tonight's performance seem more like a party . . . a party at which the guest of honor would be the president of the United States.

The second scene in the play was well underway when the players on stage suddenly halted in their paces and stepped to the front of the apron. The orchestra, under the direction of William Withers, struck up the first notes of "Hail to the Chief," and the entire audience rose to its feet.

Standing with the others, Jim and Artemus watched as the presidential party entered its box. Not counting the bodyguard, there were four people—an army major, a young woman, and the president and Mrs. Lincoln. Mrs. Lincoln was smiling broadly, whereas the president seemed somewhat preoccupied. Lincoln stepped to the railing at the front of the box, smiled, and waved to the audience with his high hat. The audience applauded appreciatively. Then, gesturing toward the stage, the president indicated that the play should continue.

Picking up the scene where it had been left off, the actor

portraying the character of Lord Dundreary spoke his next line.

"I caught a window draft, but that was cured by a doctor's draught, which I secured by issuing a bank draft."

"Good gracious," replied Laura Keene as Florence Trenchard, tossing her saucy auburn curls. "What a number of drafts! You have almost a game of drafts."

"Oh, that wath a joke, that wath," Lord Dundreary said, and the audience laughed appreciatively.

Then, Miss Keene ad-libbed, "But you need not worry now, for the draft has been suspended."

Few in the audience understood her reference, and there was an awkward pause. When the actor playing Lord Dundreary gave her a puzzled frown, indicating that he did not understand either, the actress looked directly at Lincoln and declared, pointedly, "Why . . . anybody can see that!"

Now the audience realized that she was referring to the military draft, and they roared with laughter and applauded her quick and patriotic wit. Smiling delightedly, Laura Keene momentarily interrupted the performance to take a bow. It was all great fun and enhanced the idea that the players and audience were enjoying a party. With the intimacy even more strengthened, the play continued.

Jim and Artemus's seats were in the dress circle; thus, they were at the same level as the presidential box. At a little after ten o'clock, Jim noticed someone step into the corridor that led to the box. Looking closely, he saw that it was the same actor he had met at the hotel. He leaned toward Artemus and whispered.

"I just saw Booth going toward the president's box. He must be a personal guest of the president."

"Such are the rewards of fame," Artemus replied.

"After our meeting this afternoon, I got the distinct impression that he was a southern sympathizer. It makes you wonder why he would even want to be a guest of the president," Jim mused.

On stage, the elegant, matronly character of Mrs. Mountchessington fixed Henry Hawk's crude, backwoodsman character with a meanacing glare, then hissed "I am aware, Mr. Trenchard, that you are not used to the manners of polite society." With that, she swept into the wings, leaving Henry Hawk alone on the stage.

Since many in the audience had seen the play before, they braced themselves for what they knew would be the biggest laugh in the play.

Hawk did not disappoint them. Putting his hands on his suspenders, he leaned back, peered over his shoulder, then bellowed.

"Heh, heh. Don't know the manners of good society, eh? Well, I guess I know enough to turn you inside out, old gal . . . you sockdologizing old mantrap!"

Uproarious laughter burst from the theatergoers. Because he had heard so much about the president's sense of humor, Jim looked over at Lincoln's box to see if the president had moved forward and was laughing, but he couldn't see the president's face.

At that instant he heard an ominous popping sound, even over the laughter, a sound he had heard many times during the last four years. Startled and confused at hearing that noise in a theater, he rose out of his seat and began looking around wildly. No one else in the audience, not even Artemus, seemed to have noticed.

Then Jim saw a wisp of smoke float out from the president's box. A second later, John Wilkes Booth climbed onto the railing, then leapt down onto the stage floor. One of his spurs caught on the bunting, and he fell awkwardly. Jim could tell by the way he landed that he was injured, but many in the audience, recognizing Booth as an actor and believing it to be something new in the play, laughed even louder.

"What's Booth doing there?" Artemus asked. "Something's going on."

"My God, Artie, I think Booth must've just shot the president!" Jim said.

"Stop that man!" someone shouted from the president's box. His shout was followed by a woman's scream.

On the stage, Harry Hawk was holding his hat in front

of him with both hands, his eyes open wide in surprise and fear as John Wilkes Booth rose to his feet. Booth brandished a knife above his head, glared at the audience, then shouted, ''Sic semper tyrannis!''

# 2

"Help . . . help!"

Mrs. Lincoln's voice was a shrill scream that came from the presidential box. Then she started babbling, almost insensibly, "He said they would take no notice! We were going to Egypt! The Holy Land! Please, someone help!"

Jim's first inclination was to go after Booth, but because their seats were on the dressing circle, he did not have a direct access to the stage.

"See about the president," Jim shouted. "I'm going after Booth!"

Jim ran into the corridor, then down the stairs, taking them three at a time. As he raced up the side aisle and around the orchestra pit, Jim saw the orchestra leader jump onto the stage. He also noticed that most of the theatergoers were standing in shock. The confused babble he heard told him that many still didn't know what had happened, and those who did know appeared to be waiting for someone to take charge.

By the time Jim climbed onto the stage, Harry Hawk had disappeared, but lying on the floor near the curtains at the wings was William Withers, the orchestra leader. Only Withers had physically confronted Booth, and he was wounded for his trouble. His shirtfront was splattered with blood from the knife wound.

Through a gap in the side curtains, Jim could see Booth dragging his injured leg and hurrying toward the back door of the theater. A quick glance told him that the orchestra leader wasn't that badly hurt, so Jim raced toward the back door and flung it open. Outside in the shadows of the alley, he saw Booth mounting a horse.

"Booth! Hold it right there!" Jim shouted, starting toward him.

With a glare like that of some wild animal, Booth looked at Jim, then he slapped the reins against the animal's neck. The horse was skittish and began turning in tight circles. Seizing the opportunity, Jim dashed toward the assassin, but Booth gained control of the animal just as Jim was reaching for its bridle. Jim was so agonizingly close that he could feel the leather under his fingertips, but he was unable to grab hold. Booth galloped to the end of the alley, then turned the corner.

Jim chased Booth down F Street for several blocks, cursing the fact that not only was he unmounted, but he had no gun. The actor's horse was fast, and even though Booth was injured, he was a good horseman and held the animal to a gallop.

As Booth raced through the muddy streets strewn with slippery, broken cobblestones and threaded his mount around carriages, Jim hoped that the horse would slip or stumble and throw its rider. But the surefooted animal moved quickly down the street.

Jim saw Booth turn south at the corner of Third Street, but by the time he reached the intersection, Booth was out of sight. An evening fog was rolling in, and the streetlamps were glowing eerily in the misty night.

It's fitting, he thought, that a cowardly attacker would escape on such a night.

Jim leaned against one of the lampposts, gasping for breath. Finally, he started the long walk back to the theater, sick at heart and frustrated over his inability to do anything.

•　•　•

Back in the theater, Artemus had reached the president's box at about the same time as an army doctor.

"I'm Dr. Leale," the officer said.

"Oh, Doctor," Mary Lincoln cried, her face pitiable. "Please do what you can for my dear husband. Is he dead? Can he recover?"

"I will do what I can," Dr. Leale said.

"I'm Dr. Taft, may I be of assistance?" another man asked, arriving at that time. This was a civilian.

Seeing the two doctors, Artemus realized that he might be in the way, so he stood back to watch.

"Have you found a pulse?" Dr. Taft asked.

"No, and he isn't breathing," Dr. Leale answered. Leale took a small penknife from his pocket and cut the president's coat and collar away from the shoulders and neck. Then he carefully ran his fingers through the president's hair. "Ah, here it is," he finally said.

"What have you found?" Dr. Taft asked.

"A blood clot behind the ear." He removed the clot, then probed the hole with his little finger. "My God," he said, softly. "He has a terrible wound."

"We're losing him, Doctor," Dr. Taft said urgently. "He still isn't breathing!"

Dr. Leale immediately straddled Lincoln's chest, placing his knees on either side of the president's hips. Bending forward, he opened Lincoln's mouth and pressed on his tongue, which had been blocking his windpipe. "Dr. Taft," he said, "I'm going to massage his chest. You raise and lower his arms. We must get some air into him."

Working desperately, Dr. Taft did as he was instructed. Leale began pushing his hands against Lincoln's diaphragm. The president gasped three times, then stopped. Without hesitating, Dr. Leale began mouth to mouth resuscitation.

Putting his ear to Lincoln's chest, Taft declared, "He's breathing! He's breathing, and his heart is beating."

"Thank God!" one of the onlookers exclaimed. "You have saved him."

"No," Dr. Leale said as he stood. "His wound is mortal. It is impossible for him to recover."

By the time Jim had returned to the theater, Artemus and nearly a dozen other men were carrying the gravely wounded president down the stairs. A couple of soldiers who had been in the audience took it upon themselves to open a path through the stunned and staring crowd.

Once the somber procession was outside, Dr. Leale, who was supporting Lincoln's head, glanced around the foggy, dimly lit street to determine where they could take the wounded man. Everyone was so shocked by what had happened that no one had thought about where they were going. Suddenly someone cried, "Here! Bring him in here!"

A young man holding a lit candle was standing on the stoop of Peterson's boardinghouse, located directly across the street from the theater. The candle flame bobbled as he waved, and Doctors Leale and Taft directed the bearers toward the building.

As the men started up the front steps, negotiating it by hoisting Lincoln's body high for a brief moment, Jim joined the crowd of theatergoers who were following the bearers. Artemus saw him, then walked over to join him.

"Did you catch him?"

Jim shook his head no. "I followed him for seven or eight blocks, but I was on foot and he was mounted. I didn't have a chance."

"When we spoke to Booth at the hotel, who would have thought he was planning something like this?" Artemus asked.

"We should have listened more carefully," Jim said. "His comment about which side one's sympathies were with should have given us a clue."

"After this night, my friend, there will be blame enough for all, I'm sure. We don't have to take it on ourselves." He nodded toward the boardinghouse. "Come on, let's see what is going on in there."

The two men went into the shadowy hallway, then climbed the stairs to a small room at the back of the house.

15

20128733

Standing just outside the doorway, they stared in numb disbelief at the president. He was lying motionless, and at an awkward angle on a bed that was too short for his lanky frame. The pillow beneath his head was covered with blood. The room was lighted with a single, loudly hissing gas lamp, casting a greenish glow that seemed to intensify the horror.

Suddenly there was a commotion at the front of the boardinghouse. Mrs. Lincoln, who had been sobbing uncontrollably in the theater, had just now realized that her husband had been taken away. With her face streaked with tears and her dress spattered with blood, she was led across the street. The stunned, curious theatergoers who had crowded the steps now pulled back to allow her to pass.

"Where is my dear husband?" she shouted wildly. "Where is he? Where have they taken him?"

Well-meaning people reached out to assist her, but she recoiled violently from them, as if she felt they were trying to manacle her. "What have you done with him?" she screamed, her voice growing louder as she made her way into the building and up the stairs. She finally found the room where the president lay, and she stood beside the bed, weeping and shaking as she looked down at her husband.

"Oh, somebody, please get Tad," she begged. "He will live for Tad. He will speak to him; he loves him so."

"Please find some place for Mrs. Lincoln to be comfortable," Dr. Leale said.

Jim understood that the doctor meant he did not want her in the room while they worked on the president, and he and Artemus escorted the first lady to a parlor at the front of the house. As they did, two other physicians, Doctors Barnes and King, both of whom were attached to the White House, came in and rushed up the stairs to attend the dying president.

Jim and Artemus remained in the house as the deathwatch continued. Throughout the long night, a steady procession of people, including high-ranking generals, cabinet officers, and the vice president, entered the boardinghouse. General Meigs was stationed at the front door to screen the visitors, allowing in only those with a legitimate right. Secretary of War Edwin Stanton set up his own headquarters in a room next to the one where Lincoln lay dying. While the president was drawing his last, labored breaths, the whiskered, determined Stanton was interviewing eyewitnesses and issuing orders for the capture of John Wilkes Booth.

At about three in the morning, Jim saw John Parker. By now he had learned that Parker was the man who was supposed to have been guarding the president.

"Where were you?" Jim asked, accusingly.

"Who are you?" Parker replied with a snarl. "And what business is it of yours where I was?"

"It's the business of every citizen in America to know where the man who was supposed to be guarding the president was. Now, where were you?"

"I saw the president safely to his box," Parker replied. "Then I went next door for a few minutes. I was on my way back when I saw a prostitute working the crowd in front of the theater, so I took her to jail."

"You . . . you left your post to take a prostitute to jail?" Jim asked incredulously.

"I did. I am a metropolitan policeman, after all. My first duty is to my job. Being a bodyguard was only a part-time duty. How is the president, by the way?"

"You disgust me," Jim growled. "Get out of my sight before I break every bone in your body."

"You can't talk to me that way, I told you, I'm a police officer."

"Get!" Jim shouted, and, cowering, Parker hurried away.

"I can't believe we don't have full-time bodyguards assigned to protect the president," Artemus said.

"Maybe after this, we will," Jim said.

The long night passed, and Saturday morning dawned cold, gray, and rainy. Despite the weather, a large crowd maintained a silent vigil outside the boardinghouse. Some people had been there all night and still wore the evening clothes they had donned for the theater. So many people had arrived by now that the street was packed solid with humanity for several blocks in either direction. Many were weeping, many were cursing, many more were silently praying.

At 7:22, Dr. Leale, who had held the president's head throughout the long night, noticed that Abraham Lincoln had stopped breathing. Dr. Taft placed his hand on the patient's chest, feeling for the president's heartbeat. Dr. Barnes lay his finger on the carotid artery, and Dr. Leale checked the pulse. With a sad nod, the three men then stood, and Dr. Barnes crossed the president's hands on his chest.

Secretary Edwin Stanton, his face streaked with tears, spoke the first words acknowledging the terrible truth.

"Now he belongs to the ages," he murmured.

It took Washington a week to say good-bye to the president. There were those in the government who wanted his body to remain in Washington, but in one of Mrs. Lincoln's rare rational and coherent moments, she recalled that, when Oak Ridge cemetery had opened in Springfield, Illinois, she and her husband had walked through it. He had commented then that, when his time came, he would like to rest in a place just like that.

"I want him buried there," she said.

Abraham Lincoln would be returning home to Illinois, but he wasn't going by the most direct route. Instead, plans were made to send the funeral train on a circuitous route through several of the country's biggest cities. This would give millions of people the opportunity to say a last good-bye.

When Secretary of the Treasury Hugh McCulloch asked Jim West and Artemus Gordon to come see him on the night before the train was due to leave, they were surprised to see that Secretary of War Stanton was in McCulloch's office.

Even though Stanton was in McCulloch's office, he was

still busily issuing orders. Some of the alleged conspirators in the plot to assassinate Abraham Lincoln had already been arrested, and there were reports that John Wilkes Booth had been seen in Maryland.

"I want hourly reports," Stanton was saying to one of the men hovering around him. "Do you understand? Even if there is nothing to report, I want to hear it hourly."

"Yes, Mr. Secretary."

"Edwin," McCulloch said. "These are the two men I told you about—James West and Artemus Gordon."

Stanton looked at them for a moment. "I'm told you almost caught Booth," he said.

"I chased him," Jim replied. "Unfortunately, I didn't catch him."

Stanton stroked his beard. "Yes, well, even if you had, it would have been like shutting the barn door after the horse was gone. We should have guarded the president more diligently while he was alive."

"Yes, sir, my sentiments exactly," Jim said.

"The problem is that we have no means of doing that, unless we surround our president with soldiers. And I don't think our country is ready for something like a Praetorian guard."

"No, sir, perhaps not," Jim replied, not entirely sure where the conversation was going.

"Hugh has suggested that the mission of the Secret Service could be expanded to include guarding the president. What would you think about that?"

"I think it would be a good idea," Jim said.

"You are a national police service. And you would be in civilian clothes, rather than in military uniforms."

"Edwin, I agree with you one hundred percent," Mc-Culloch said. "But I would remind you that, though we have started preliminary operations, we don't yet exist, technically. The bill had not yet been presented to the president for signing. And even if we are approved, our mission is very narrowly defined. We are in business to control counterfeiting."

"Yes, but, you are a *secret* service, aren't you? Is it not possible that certain agents could be given specific . . . secret . . . instructions?''

"I'm sure that would be possible,'' McCulloch replied.

"Good. Then I'm asking you to give such instructions to these two men, now. I want them to guard President Lincoln.''

"I beg your pardon, sir? Guard President Lincoln?'' Jim asked.

"Yes. Or, rather, his body,'' Stanton said. "A Confederate general named Culpepper has just come to us with the information that there is a plot to steal the president's body. He has had a change of heart and no longer wants anything to do with it.''

"How good is his information?'' Jim asked.

"Very good, I would say,'' Stanton replied. "Seeing as how he is the one who instigated the plan. On top of everything else our country has had to go through lately, to have the president's body stolen would be a devastating blow.''

"Yes, I can see that it would be very traumatic,'' Artemus agreed.

"But I don't understand. What possible reason would anyone have for stealing the president's body?'' McCulloch asked.

"I believe General Culpepper had some idea of forcing more favorable terms for the defeated South.''

"Why would he come to you now?''

"According to Culpepper, he has been swept up in the outpouring of grief. It has, he claims, made him reevaluate the situation.''

"If he has reevaluated, why doesn't he just cancel the operation?'' Jim asked.

"It is too late for him to cancel. He has already sent three of his best officers out to accomplish the task. The three officers are Colonel Nelson Bailey, Captain Reeves Purvis, and Lieutenant Gerald Meeker. They are, to quote General Culpepper, 'totally dedicated to their mission.' They won't stop, so they will have to *be* stopped.''

"What do you want with my agents?'' McCulloch asked.

"What I am suggesting, Mr. Secretary, is that you assign

the two of them to ride on the funeral train for the president's entire journey back to Illinois," Stanton said. "If any attempt is made to steal the president's body, they are to stop it."

McCulloch nodded. "Gentlemen, you may consider yourselves on loan to Secretary Stanton," McCulloch said.

"Very good, sir," Jim replied.

At six o'clock on the morning of Friday, April 21, Jim West, Artemus Gordon, and three hundred carefully selected passengers stood waiting on the Baltimore and Ohio station platform beside the funeral train. Among the senators, congressmen, and dignitaries making the journey were the president's two brothers-in-law from Springfield; two first cousins of Mrs. Lincoln; Dr. Phineas Gurley, a Presbyterian pastor; Dr. Brown, the embalmer; and Thomas Pendel, the White House doorkeeper.

A cold drizzle was falling, but the overhanging roof of the platform sheltered the passengers as they stood waiting for the hearse that bore the slain president's body. A few minutes earlier, in a discreet but solemn ceremony, a small casket had been loaded onto the funeral car.

"What is that?" Artemus asked. "It looks like a coffin, but it is much too small to be the president's."

Although Secretary McCulloch wouldn't be making the trip, he was there to see his two agents off.

"It is the president's son, Willie," McCulloch explained. "It was the family's wish that Willie be returned to Springfield to be buried with his father."

The engineer had already built up the steam pressure in the locomotive as it waited with its string of nine cars for the somber cargo. The relief valve was opening and closing rhythmically as it vented excess pressure, producing what Jim thought was almost a sobbing sound.

To prepare for the solemn occasion, the engine had been cleaned meticulously, its brass fittings polished to a high shine, and then heavily draped in black crepe. The American flags fitted to the top of the cowcatcher to protrude on either side of the boiler provided the only touch of color.

On the front of the boiler was a wreath that encircled a large, black-bordered picture of the president.

Jim heard the heavy boom of a distant cannon. That was the signal that the funeral cortege had just departed from the White House to begin its stately procession up Pennsylvania Avenue toward the depot. When he had ridden to the station at dawn, he had not been surprised to see that, despite the early hour, thousands of people were already standing on each side of the avenue, weeping and waiting to say one last good-bye to their slain leader.

The first thing Jim and Artemus did when they arrived at the depot was to examine the car Lincoln's body would ride in. The car, the last of nine cars, had been specifically built to be used by the president of the United States during his official travels. As fate had it, this would be the first and only time President Lincoln would ever ride in the car.

The original design called for the car to be divided into three sections: a bedroom, a sitting room, and a dining area. For this somber journey, the sections had been converted. The front section now provided seating for the honor guard. In the larger, middle section, stood the bier on which the president's coffin would lie; and the rear section, the smallest of the three compartments, housed the coffin bearing Willie. When Jim and Artemus looked inside the car, the middle section was stark and empty; but when they looked into the rear compartment, they saw Willie's coffin.

The inside walls, floor, and ceiling of the car, which had been covered in a rich, maroon tapestry, were now veiled by heavy black drapery. On the presidential bier was a black pall fringed with knotted tassels. Next to the catafalque were two empty chairs, one on each side. During the trip, one of these chairs would be occupied by Admiral Charles Davis, representing the navy, and the other by General Edward Townsend, who would represent the army.

When Jim and Artemus returned to the platform, they could hear the muffled thump of drums growing louder, signaling the approach of the funeral procession.

"Where are Mrs. Lincoln, and the president's son, Robert?" Artemus asked.

"Neither one of them will be on the funeral train," McCulloch replied. "Mrs. Lincoln has refused to attend the funeral, and Robert is going to remain in Washington until the last possible moment. Then he will take a fast train, and arrive in Springfield ahead of the funeral train."

The sound of the drums was so loud now, that it was clear the cortege had arrived in the station. Jim and Artemus watched as the cortege moved onto the platform. Then Dr. Phineas Gurley, the pastor, stepped to the head of the coffin to offer a prayer while all present removed their hats and bowed their heads.

"Watch over this sleeping dust of our fallen chief magistrate as it passes from our view and is borne to its final resting place in the soil of that state which was his abiding and chosen home," Dr. Gurley prayed.

As soon as Dr. Gurley uttered the last syllable of his prayer, the engine's bell began to clang. The sound came so quickly that Jim suspected the engineer had been irreverent enough to have had his hand on the cord throughout the prayer. Smoke began belching from the wide-mouthed stack even as the conductor and other officials quickly ushered the passengers aboard. Moments later, the funeral train inched away from the platform and out of the depot.

As the train rolled out of the depot, it passed between two lines of black soldiers. They were from a regiment which, because of their race, had not been allowed to enter the depot. The soldiers chose to pay their respects in this way. They stood lined up alongside the tracks, standing rigidly at attention, their grief evident on their tear-stained faces. As the train passed the soldiers, Jim thought he had never seen a more moving tribute.

# 3

When the train left Harrisburg, Pennsylvania, the rain that had plagued them for two days was at last over. As they rolled through towns and cities, Jim saw that thousands of people were drawn to the trackside, even though the train would not be stopping. At one point he saw a big sign that read: ABRAHAM LINCOLN, THE ILLUSTRIOUS MARTYR OF LIBERTY, THE NATION MOURNS HIS LOSS. THOUGH DEAD, HE STILL LIVES.

At Lancaster, Artemus pointed to an old man who was sitting in a buggy at the depot, his hat held respectfully in his hands as the train rolled without stopping through the station.

"Is that who I think it is?" Artemus asked.

Jim looked at the man Artemus had pointed out. "Yes. That's former President Buchanan."

As the train continued on its journey, Jim was struck with scenes that he knew would stay in his memory for the rest of his life. Shops and factories were closed, and the population of every town and village along the way was turned out beside the tracks to stand or, in many cases, to kneel, in silence. Once he spotted a solitary farmer at work behind his plow on a far, lonely hill. As the train neared, the distant figure knelt and bowed his head.

The closer the train got to Philadelphia, the larger the crowds were. It was still several miles from the city limits when Jim realized there were no gaps at all along the tracks—just solid lines of humanity. The train arrived in Philadelphia at the Broad Street station at half past four. As with the other cities, Philadelphia would have its own funeral. With great pomp and ceremony, the honor guard loaded Lincoln's coffin onto the waiting hearse, which was draped in black and white and crowned with three enormous white plumes that waved at the top of the canopy. Eight black horses, their coats gleaming in the sun, pulled Lincoln's body toward Independence Square. Booming cannons and tolling bells announced the departure of the hearse from the station.

Much to the dismay of Philadelphia city officials, plans for a dignified funeral were marred by a near-riot. The police, perhaps overreacting, charged into the crowd, shoving people back and hitting them with nightsticks when necessary to restore order. One man was killed in the melee.

The crowd was even larger in New York, but, the newspapers reported glowingly, the citizens of New York were well-behaved, so the unpleasantness that had plagued Philadelphia was avoided.

*Port Royal, Virginia, Sixty Miles from Washington, D.C.*

While the nation was distracted by the westward journey of the funeral train, a detachment of twenty-five soldiers tracked the assassin, John Wilkes Booth, to a tobacco barn at the Garrert farm near Port Royal, Virginia. When Booth refused to come out, the barn was set ablaze. As it was burning, one of the soldiers, Sergeant Boston Corbett, stepped up to the barn, put the muzzle of his rifle between the cracks of the boards, and pulled the trigger. His bullet struck Booth in the back of the head, in almost exactly the same place Lincoln had been hit. When Booth fell, several soldiers rushed into the burning barn and dragged him out.

Two and a half hours later, the man Boston Corbett had shot died. The body was taken to Alexandria on board the steamer *John S. Ide*, then by tugboat across the Potomac to the Washington navy yard. There, it was placed on a carpenter's bench. Ten witnesses who knew Booth on sight were summoned to identify him.

His appearance was greatly changed: his face was shriveled and yellow from exposure and starvation, and contorted with the pain he had experienced with his broken leg. His mustache had been shaven off and his face was covered with an eleven-day-old beard.

At first, none of the ten men thought the body bore any resemblance to the actor, but eventually, and with varying degrees of conviction, they decided that the body they were viewing was, indeed, that of John Wilkes Booth. Accordingly, he was identified as such.

On the night of April 27, in stark contrast to the stately funeral by which the nation was saying a long good-bye to the president, Booth's body was spirited out in the dark of the night. The corpse was sewn in a tarpaulin and put into a wooden guncase. It was then buried under the brick floor of what had been the dining room of the old penitentiary on the Washington side of the arsenal grounds. Thus the assassin was buried, even before his victim.

*On Board the Funeral Train*

The riot in Philadelphia caused Jim and Artemus to change the way they were performing their duty. Instead of both riding on the train with the president's body, Jim went ahead of the train on a pilot engine, keeping his eyes open for anything that might be a little unusual.

He arrived in Cardington, Ohio at three o'clock in the morning, approximately two hours before the funeral train was scheduled to pass through. Even though it was the middle of the night and no stop was planned, several hundred mourners were gathered along the tracks.

Jim looked at all the people who were standing in the glow, waiting for the train. There were very old people and very young children, prosperous businessmen and poor farmers, beautiful young ladies and women whose clothes and features bore the mark of years of hard work. There were soldiers and ex-soldiers, some in uniforms that were little more than tattered rags, evidence of years of hard campaigning. Some of the soldiers had empty sleeves and trouser legs, having left a limb at such places as Shiloh, Gettysburg, and the wilderness. But here, in the flickering light of torches and bonfires, all were joined by their common sorrow over Lincoln's death.

Jim dismounted, tied his horse to a rail behind the depot, and went inside the building. He was surprised to see that the lunch counter was open. It would normally be closed at this hour, but the enterprising proprietor had apparently decided to take advantage of the crowd. However, it appeared that very few people were willing to pay five cents for a cup of coffee or a sandwich. Except for two patrons, the counter was empty. The proprietor was obviously disappointed by his lack of business, because when Jim stepped up to buy a cup of coffee, he seemed to find it an imposition, and he served it listlessly.

Jim looked at the other two customers and saw from their uniforms that one was the stationmaster and the other was the telegrapher. They were sitting at the end, talking together. Picking up his cup and moving down the counter to join them, Jim said to the telegrapher, "Excuse me, sir, my name is Jim West. Do you have any messages for me?"

"West? No, I don't think so," he replied. "Why, should I?"

"Not necessarily," Jim said. "But I am with the United States government, assigned to protect the president's funeral train. I'm traveling ahead of the train while my partner stays on board. I thought he might have wired me."

"I've received nothing," the telegrapher said.

"Why would you need to protect the funeral train?" the stationmaster asked.

"It's just a precaution," Jim said. He didn't share with

27

them the threat to steal the president's body.

The stationmaster pulled out his watch and looked at it. "One hour and forty-five minutes before the train comes through," he announced.

"Maybe when the officials on the train see so many people waiting here, they'll stop," the telegrapher suggested.

"No, no, they are on a very strict schedule," the stationmaster replied.

"I hate to keep bothering you," Jim said, interrupting their discussion. "But has anyone come through here who might have caught your attention? Anything out of the ordinary?"

"Are you kidding, mister?" the stationmaster replied. "Look at the people out there! There's nothing at all usual about this night. What are you looking for, anyway?"

"I'm not sure what I'm looking for," Jim admitted.

"If you don't know what you are looking for, how can we help you?"

"What about that stolen engine?" the telegrapher asked. "That seems pretty unusual, doesn't it?"

"Someone has stolen an engine?" Jim asked.

The telegrapher nodded. "And a tender," he said. "There were three of them in on it. The stationmaster over in Marysville thought they might be soldiers. Leastwise, he said they acted like soldiers. Thing is, nobody can figure out why anyone would want an engine."

"It has to be Colonel Bailey," Jim said.

"Beg your pardon?"

"Never mind, I was just thinking out loud. Do you have a map?" Jim asked.

"Yes, over there on the wall. There's a big one of the whole state of Ohio. Every railroad is clearly marked."

Hurrying across the room, Jim studied the map. He quickly located Marysville, then north and south switch, all a few miles south of Cardington. He put one finger on north switch and another on south switch, then let out a long, slow sigh.

"Colonel Bailey, I hope you aren't planning to do what I think you are planning to do."

"Did you say something, Mister?" the stationmaster called, hearing Jim mumble.

"No," Jim answered, still studying the map.

"Well, if you're plannin' to watch the funeral train come through, you'd best get out there and find yourself a good place to stand. Folks are still comin' from all around, and pretty soon all the good places will be taken."

The telegraph instrument suddenly started clacking, and the telegrapher went over to read it.

"What is it?" the stationmaster asked.

"It's Marcus Pell over in Marian. He wants to know if he can let the eastbound freight pass."

The stationmaster looked at his watch. "Tell him to let it go through," he said. "But don't let anything else through until after the funeral train is safely by."

Jim looked at the stationmaster and telegrapher. "You mean you have a freight coming through here?"

"In about half an hour," the stationmaster said with a nod. "Actually, it'll just be crossin' the main line about a mile north of here. It's a good thing, too. If it came through the station, most of the folks would think it was the funeral train instead of nothin' but empty boxcars."

Jim turned back to examine the map again and found the cross track the stationmaster had spoken of. Three men had stolen an engine and tender. Why would someone do that? Nobody would do it unless they were planning something . . . something that had to do with the funeral train. It had to be Bailey and his men.

Jim thought for a long moment. Half a dozen scenarios came to mind, from using the stolen train to make a rapid getaway once the body was stolen to crashing the engine into the funeral train. Although he had nothing but a hunch to go on, the consequences of such a thing actually happening were so bad that he felt he had no choice but to act on his hunch. He nodded his head, silently making up his mind to act. There was no way to explain what he was about to do. If he had guessed wrong, he would be committing a criminal act. But if his hunch was right, he might

29

just be preventing the theft of what was, for the moment, the nation's most sacred icon.

On board the funeral train, a dim lantern burned at each end of the car in which Artemus was riding. The light wasn't bright enough to allow him to see much, but it did provide enough illumination for him to walk the length of the car without tripping.

It was quiet in the car. All he could hear was the normal rush and rhythmic click of the train traversing the rails. He glanced up and down the aisle and saw only the shadowy, dark-green drapes that hung over the berths behind which slept thirty-nine other passengers. Beneath the lantern at the rear of the car, he saw the porter sitting in a chair that was tipped back against the wall. His hands were folded in his lap, and his chin was down on his chest. He, too, was sleeping.

Artemus moved noiselessly toward the rear, slipped past the porter, and left the car. Then he walked through the next two cars, which were equally dark and quiet, and continued on until he reached the last car on the train.

As Artemus tiptoed through the front section of the last car, he heard the gentle snoring and even breathing of the general and admiral who were sleeping there. The middle section was brightly lit, and even though he had looked in here half a dozen times, something compelled him to step in again.

The coffin lid was normally closed while the train was underway. Tonight, however, it was open, and he discovered that he was staring right into Lincoln's face. He peered at him more closely than he had at any other time. Lincoln's mouth was curled into the slightest suggestion of a smile.

Jim had confessed to Artemus that he had never seen the president in person, until that night at the Ford Theater. He had seen pictures of him, and from those photographs, thought Lincoln to be a homely man. He'd mentioned that to Artemus, and Artemus discredited the pictures, saying, "No photograph could ever catch the infinite gradations of expression that passed over Lincoln's face each moment.

Homely? Abraham Lincoln is one of the handsomest men I have ever seen.''

In death, those gradations of expression could no longer manifest themselves on the president's face. But, even now, Artemus could see that the gentleness had remained.

## Cardington Depot

Jim West dashed out of the Cardington depot and onto the station platform. At the far end of the platform, he spotted the shadowy outline of what he was looking for—a storage shed—and he smiled. Walking quickly to the shed, he paused and looked over his shoulder at the darkened outlines of hundreds of people standing along the track waiting for the funeral train. As he had expected, everyone was staring down the track, watching anxiously for the first glimpse of the president's train.

Jim sneaked into the shed, lit a lantern, then used it to look around until he found what he needed: a box of railroad torpedoes. Placed on railroad tracks, the torpedoes would detonate when the wheels of an engine rode over them. The resulting noise was a signal to the engineer to make an emergency stop. That was exactly what Jim hoped to accomplish.

Grabbing three torpedoes, Jim slipped them into his pocket, extinguished the lantern, and left the shed. Leaving his horse tethered at the depot, he ran as quickly as he could along the twin lines of glimmering steel to the railroad junction one mile north of the station. He was relieved that it was far enough way from the depot and not on the main track, so that no one waiting to watch the funeral train pass would witness what he was going to do.

His pulse hammering in his head from the exertion of his run, he forced himself to breathe deeply and calm down. As his control returned, he scanned the countryside and listened intently. It was still quite dark, and the sounds of night creatures—frogs, crickets, an owl—were all he heard at first. Then another sound echoing in the distance reached him. It was the chugging of a steam engine, and he realized it had to be the eastbound freight.

Jim ran about a quarter of a mile up the cross track, then spread the three torpedoes out on the rail. Even as he worked, he could see the beam of the approaching head-lamp stabbing through the night and hear the mournful sound of the whistle as the train drew closer. With the torpedoes in place, he scrambled away from the track into a clump of brush and watched the train approach.

Three sharp bangs sounded over the clatter of the train as the wheels hit the torpedoes. Almost immediately the brakes squealed and shrieked as steel slid on steel in a shower of sparks.

Jim stayed out of sight until the engine came to a halt, and the engineer and fireman climbed down from the cab to see what was wrong. From his hiding place, Jim could clearly hear them talking to each other.

"What do you think it was?" the engineer asked.

"Well, it has to be that funeral train," his fireman replied. "But I thought we'd been given the go-ahead on that."

"Maybe they speeded up the train."

The fireman pushed back his cap and scratched his forehead. "Then where is it? I sure don't see no lights, and I don't hear nothin', either."

Jim stepped out of his hiding place and walked toward the two men. "I'm sorry, gentlemen. I stopped your train."

The startled engineer jumped slightly, then whirled around to face Jim, illuminated by the glow of the head-lamp. "You stopped it? Why, man?" The engineer glared. "This is no time for some fool joke."

"I assure you, I'm not joking," Jim said coldly. He pulled his pistol.

Dumbfounded, the two men immediately raised their hands. "Don't shoot us!" the fireman pleaded.

"I won't if you do as I say," the agent answered.

"Mister, you must be plumb crazy trying to rob this

train,'' the engineer growled. ''We're not hauling anything but a string of empty boxcars.''

''Disconnect your engine and tender from the cars,'' Jim ordered.

''What?''

''All I want is your engine and tender. Disconnect it, please,'' Jim repeated.

Five minutes later, with the engine disconnected from the rest of the train, Jim climbed into the cab where the hissing sound of steam and the dial on the gage, illuminated by the cab's lantern, told him that the pressure was still high enough for him to make it move. He took one last glance at the two nervous trainmen, then opened the throttle. The engine began rolling.

The last thing Jim had done prior to stopping the freight train was to set the switch at the junction so that, rather than cross the main line, his engine would turn south onto it.

Minutes later, the engine Jim was driving pounded through the station at Cardington where the hundreds of people lining the platform all assumed it was the pilot engine for the funeral train. Within a few more moments he was away from Cardington, headed toward north switch.

At north switch, Jim applied the brakes and the engine rolled to a stop. He stuck his head out and looked up and down the track, but saw no sign of any other train. Where was Colonel Bailey? Was he on the main line, or on the line headed for Marysville?

''Marysville,'' Jim decided, saying the name aloud.

Having no time to second-guess himself, he immediately hopped down and turned the switch bar that would allow him to leave the main track. Then he climbed back into the engine, released the brake, and started rolling forward. As soon as the back wheels had cleared the switching point, he stopped the engine and ran to the switch bar to close it. Then he hurried back to the cab and started toward Marysville.

Less than five minutes later, he saw the approaching headlight of an engine and realized that it was going the wrong way on the track headed for north switch.

He had guessed right! Bailey was planning to intercept the funeral train. For a moment, Jim wasn't sure what to do. Then a cold, calm understanding passed over him.

After first checking the steam pressure, Jim threw several more logs onto the fire to keep it roaring and to keep the pressure up. That done, he opened the throttle to full.

With the train racing along the track toward the oncoming headlight, Jim climbed down the cab's steps and hung on. He looked at the ground rushing beneath him, moving so fast that it was a blur. Then, steeling himself, he took a deep breath and pushed himself away from the engine, leaping as far as he could. He hit the ground with a bone-jarring thud, then tumbled and bounced painfully for several yards. Finally, he rolled to a stop. Although every part of his body ached, he was sure nothing was broken. Pulling himself to his feet, he watched, his heart pounding, as the two engines raced toward each other. The wrenching, shrieking sound of steel battering steel shattered the still night. Then a mighty explosion shook the ground as both boilers exploded. A great column of steam, so white as to be fluorescent, roared into the darkened sky, and a scalding rain began to fall. Huge metal parts were flung into the air, then crashed back to the ground with the force of an artillery barrage.

When the last piece of shrapnel had fallen and it was safe to stand again, Jim hauled himself out of the clump of bushes he had dived into for cover and looked at the mangled mountain of steel. The shower of hot water had extinguished the boilers' flames, so there was no fire. Shattered boilers, crushed smokestacks, crumpled tenders, and broken wheels resting on twisted track were all that remained of the two great engines. Only the hissing steam still trapped in the cylinders, and the snapping and popping of cooling metal could be heard in the night.

Pulling his gun, Jim moved slowly toward the wreck. He circled it warily, then checked the entire area. He could find neither survivors nor dead men. Colonel Bailey and his men had gotten away. But at least their plan to intercept the funeral train had been foiled.

34

# 4

After what had seemed to be two weeks of continuous rain, Thursday, May 4, dawned sunny and bright in Springfield, Illinois. It was also blistering hot. To start the ceremonies, thirty-six guns were fired in salute, then a single gun was fired at ten-minute intervals throughout the morning until the funeral cortege was ready to begin its two-mile journey to the cemetery.

A detail of veteran sergeants carried the coffin from the statehouse rotunda and slid it reverently into a special hearse that was on loan to Springfield from the city of St. Louis. Then, escorted by a military guard of one thousand members, the funeral procession began its final march. In the hot air, heavy with the scent of lilacs, it wound through the streets of Springfield, then traveled down a country road to the cemetery.

Even though thousands marched or rode in the parade, no one spoke. The only sounds were the hollow clomping of the horses' hooves, the rumble of the wheels, the tramp of the soldiers' feet, and the steady, muffled beat of drums that matched the rhythm of a heartbeat—a muted thump, thump, thump.

Finally, the procession passed under the evergreen arch at the cemetery entrance and moved through the little valley between two tree-covered ridges to a receiving vault that had been dug into the hillside. Here, Lincoln's body was placed in a public tomb where it would lie until his own grand sepulcher could be constructed.

By noon the ceremony was over, and the nation's long good-bye had been said. Jim West and Artemus Gordon, their first mission successfully completed, telegraphed Secretary McCulloch for their next assignment.

They were surprised by the answer they received.

"General Culpepper believes that Colonel Bailey and his men will make one final attempt to steal the body tonight from the crypt. Recommend you maintain watch for twenty-four more hours."

After sunset on the day of Lincoln's interment, heavy clouds began rolling in to blot out the moon and the stars. The cemetery was not lit by torches or gaslights, and it was so dark that it was impossible to see for more than a few feet.

"I wonder if we should move closer," Artemus whispered to Jim.

"This is as close as we can get and still have some cover," Jim replied. "Besides, if Bailey is actually going to try this, they'll be just as blind as we are. If they're going to be successful in removing the body, they'll have to have a light of some kind. When they arrive, we'll be sure to see them."

The wait seemed interminable. Unable to see anything, Jim felt as if they were inside a dark tunnel. Suddenly a white light blinded him. A thunderstorm was brewing. Every few seconds a jagged streak of lightning flashed across the sky, momentarily revealing the details of the cemetery in a harsh, brilliant glare that hurt the eyes before blackness returned. Seconds after each stark white flash, thunder boomed loudly, roaring like the ceremonial cannons that had been fired to honor the fallen president over the last twenty days.

With each lightning flash the tombstones were eerily highlighted, and long, ghostly shadows were cast over the scene. Suddenly the wind picked up, rustling and blowing the branches over their heads and making it hard to hear anything else. Drops of rain began pelting them, and Jim and Artemus hunkered down like turtles retreating into their shells.

Jim wondered if Colonel Bailey and his men would show up on such a night. Curious to know just how long they had been waiting, he took out his watch and held it up so that he would be able to read the face during the next lightning flash. But Jim did not learn what time it was.

When the next bolt of lightning streaked across the sky, he saw three men stealthily approaching the tomb. Keeping his eyes riveted on them so he would know where they were when the blackness descended again, he slid his watch back into his pocket. One of the men was carrying a lantern, although the light was so carefully shielded that the flame was barely visible.

"There they are," Jim hissed urgently, nudging Artemus and pointing to the pinpoint of moving light.

Lightning flashed again, illuminating the trio in its stark glare.

"Colonel Bailey! Captain Purvis! Lieutenant Meeker! Hold it right there! You are covered!" Jim shouted.

"Colonel! They know our names!" a frightened voice called.

"Quiet!" Bailey shouted back.

Blackness erased the image. The lantern was quickly extinguished, but not before Jim had made a mental note of where it was located. There was a flash of gunfire as one of the three men fired his pistol toward Jim and Artemus. Though the man was just guessing as to where Jim might be, he was surprisingly close because Jim heard the bullet whine into the trees.

Jim returned fire, shooting into the darkness at the flame that had spat from the rebel's gun. But the next bolt of lightning revealed that the three Confederate officers had disappeared.

Another gunshot rang out. This time the bullet whistled into the trees above their heads and Jim and Artemus realized that their position was too vulnerable. He and Artemus split up, each going in a different direction and firing as he ran.

The roaring of guns joined the flashing lightning and booming thunder, making the small cemetery seem more like a battlefield than a place of peaceful, eternal repose. Jim felt a sense of unreality, as if the gunfight were something he was dreaming. The harsh flashes of the lightning dimmed his vision, and the ever-moving shadows cast by tree branches would have made it virtually impossible to spot his targets, were it not for the orange flames that spat from their pistols.

The would-be grave robbers knew how to fire and move, fire and move—never giving their enemies a stationary target. They kept up a steady barrage of shots, and the lead flew through the night air, whining off the marble gravestones and whistling through the trees.

Then Jim fired at one of the orange flames too quickly for the robber to move away, and his bullet found its mark. He heard a gasp, then a cry of pain.

For a moment everyone stopped shooting.

"Give it up, men! We've got you covered!" Jim shouted.

One of the three robbers called to his accomplice. "Colonel Bailey, they got Lieutenant Meeker. What'll we do?"

For answer, Colonel Bailey fired toward Jim. Then he shouted, "We fight, Captain Purvis. We fight!"

Jim fired back in the direction of the shot, and he heard a scream.

"Colonel! Colonel Bailey, did he get you?" Captain Purvis shouted. "Colonel, answer me!"

At first there was no response, then Bailey groaned. "I'm hit."

"You're hit and Meeker's dead. What'll we do now?"

"You will have to assume command of the operation," Colonel Bailey said.

"Give it up, Colonel Bailey," Jim called again. "It's all over."

"What's over?" Colonel Bailey called back.

38

"General Culpepper has called off the mission."

There was a moment of silence, then Bailey said, "How do we know that?"

"How else would we have known about it?" Jim replied. "How would we have known your names? The war's over, gentlemen. Let this end, now."

"What will happen to us if we do?" Colonel Bailey asked.

"Nothing," Jim called. "Come out here and drop your guns, then go home."

"Go home? Just like that?"

"Just like that," Jim said.

There was a long period of silence, then two men appeared. At first, they were just darker shadows in the night, then there was an illuminating flash of lightning. In the flash of light, Jim could see that one of the men was holding both hands up, but the other had only one arm lifted. His left was dangling by his side.

"You are Colonel Bailey?" Jim said to the wounded man.

"I am, sir. And you are?"

"Captain James West," Jim said, thinking that, for the moment, it would be better to revert to his former military status.

The storm had abated, and it seemed to Jim that the cessation of the fireworks overhead had managed, somehow, to coincide with the peace achieved below. A few, far-off lightning flashes continued to provide periodic illumination of the scene.

"How badly are you hurt?" Jim asked.

"I don't think it's too bad," Bailey said. "Are you telling the truth? You've spoken to Culpepper?"

"Yes. He surrendered himself, then told about this operation."

"So, too late, the general has second thoughts," Bailey scoffed. "Too bad he couldn't have come to this decision before we started. If he had, Lieutenant Meeker would still be alive."

"I'm sorry," Jim said. "But the general had no way of

getting word to you. And when the shooting started, we had no choice but to return fire."

"I'm not blaming you, Captain," Bailey said. "You were only doing your duty. As were we," he added.

"I believe you said something about our going home?" Captain Purvis questioned.

"Yes. I am willing to parole you, if you will accept it."

"And, just what are the conditions of our parole?" Colonel Bailey asked.

"There is only one condition," Jim replied. "You must never tell anyone what happened here tonight. The world must never learn of the attempt to steal Abraham Lincoln's body."

"That is all that is required of us?"

"That is all."

"Then you have my word on it, sir," Colonel Bailey said. "No one will ever hear of this."

"You have my word as well," Captain Purvis agreed.

Suddenly another bolt of lightning cast its glare in a much brighter flash than those of a moment earlier. Something stark and gaunt loomed beside Lincoln's tomb. It looked like a very tall man wearing a top hat. Colonel Bailey gasped. Then a second lightning flash revealed that it was merely the tall stump of a dead tree.

Laughing uneasily, Bailey murmured, "For a moment I thought Lincoln was still with us."

"He is," Jim said gently. "And I have a feeling he always will be."

# 5

*Denver, Colorado*
*Sixteen Years Later*

A private railcar sat on a siding in Denver, Colorado. China, crystal, and silver gleamed from the table where Secret Service agent Jim West was seated between two very attractive women. Jim's partner, Artemus, was standing over a chafing dish. They had just finished an elaborate meal, and Artemus was about to prepare a dessert flambé.

"Get ready," Artemus said. He poured the brandy, then ignited it. A perfectly controlled blue flame erupted.

"Oh, how wonderful!" Kay said, clapping her hands in delight.

"I would be frightened to try that, for fear of setting something on fire," Linda said.

"There is nothing to it, ladies," Artemus said. "All it requires is skill, dexterity, and focus."

"And an occasional towel," Jim said.

"A towel?" Linda asked.

"All right, one time I needed a towel, and you won't let me forget it," Artemus said.

"I don't understand. Why would you need a towel?" Linda asked.

"He didn't need it; the wife of the lieutenant governor of Wyoming needed it," Jim said. "She got wet."

"What does that have to do with a flambé?" Kay asked.

"Because someone left the window open," Artemus explained.

"Oh, I see. And the rain came in," Kay said.

"No, it wasn't raining," Jim said.

"Then how did the wife of the lieutenant governor get wet?"

"Because the breeze lifted the curtain," Artemus continued as he served up the dessert.

"Which got into the flames," Jim added. "Uhmm, delicious, Professor Gordon."

"Thank you, Mr. West."

"Then what happened?" Kay asked.

"Oh. Well, the carpet was ruined," Artemus said.

"Carpet?" Linda asked. "I thought it was the curtains. What happened to the carpet?"

"The ceiling fell on it," Jim said.

"Well, of course the ceiling fell on it, Jim," Artemus said. "When the walls cave in, the ceiling is naturally going to come crashing down."

"Oh, my! The walls caved in?" Kay asked.

"Well, not right away. Not until they were weakened by the fire."

"It wasn't just a little fire, I take it?" Linda asked.

Jim laughed. "Hardly. The newspaper claimed it was the biggest fire they had ever had in Cheyenne."

"One of the pumpers worked so hard that it sprung a leak and water spewed out everywhere," Artemus said.

"Absolutely soaking the lieutenant governor's wife," Jim added.

"Which is the one and only time I've ever needed a towel to make my dessert flambé," Artemus concluded.

The women laughed at the story, not certain whether or not they should even believe it.

"Ladies, a toast," Artemus said, hoisting his glass. "To two of the loveliest ladies I have ever encountered. And, as an old thespian myself, may I say that I found your dance of the veils particularly charming.''

"You *are* an actor, aren't you?" Kay asked. "I knew there was something about you. You have a certain . . . presence."

Artemus preened and smiled at Jim. "Yes, well, some of us do have it."

Jim chuckled. "Indeed, Artie, and you have a great deal of it," he teased.

"Speaking of actors, did either of you see the article in the paper about John Wilkes Booth?"

"You mean Edwin, don't you?" Artemus said. "Edwin is John Wilkes Booth's brother, and a nicer, and more talented man you would never hope to meet. He can't be held responsible for the sin of his brother."

Linda shook her head. "No, I mean John Wilkes Booth, the man who killed Lincoln. I was very young then, but I remember how sad everyone was when it happened."

"What about John Wilkes Booth?" Jim asked.

"According to the article in the paper, John Wilkes Booth isn't dead."

"Don't be silly. Of course he is dead," Kay said.

"I didn't say he wasn't," Linda replied. "I'm just telling you what it said in the paper. It was in today's paper. Do you have a copy?"

"We do, as a matter of fact," Artemus said. "I just haven't had the opportunity to look at it."

"It's on page three," Linda said.

Artemus opened the paper to page three, looked at it for a moment, then nodded. "Here it is."

Artemus began to read aloud: "Assassin said to have been seen in Texas. News has reached us from Texas that someone claims to have seen John Wilkes Booth. This is not an apparition, such as Banquo's ghost, a character in the Shakespearean dramas Booth used to play, but it is being passed off as an actual sighting.

"Thomas Gilstrap, who claims that he was an acquaintance of John Wilkes Booth years ago, has expressed the belief that the man he saw, though older, and wearing a

43

beard, is the same man. In making his report, Mr. Gilstrap also submitted a claim for the reward that was posted for Booth immediately after the assassination.''

''What did I tell you?'' Kay asked.

Aretmus put the paper down. ''It's just a creative way to try and claim the reward.''

''There is a reward?'' Linda asked.

''There was,'' Jim said. ''But it has already been paid out. It was divided among the soldiers who actually found him.''

''If the man the soldiers found really was John Wilkes Booth,'' Linda said. ''What if it wasn't?''

''Trust me, ladies . . . the man the soldiers found was John Wilkes Booth,'' Artemus said.


*Nolan County, Texas*

A group of horsemen, eerily illuminated by the flickering torches many of them were carrying, appeared on the crest of the hill that overlooked the Montoya Ranch. The leader of the group looked down on the collection of buildings.

''Juan Montoya,'' the leader said under his breath. ''You should have gone back to Mexico when you had your chance.''

''He couldn't have gone back to Mexico,'' one of the near riders said. He pointed to the group of buildings. ''This here ranch has been here since before Texas broke away from the Mexicans.''

''All the more reason he should have left,'' the leader said. ''When we gained our independence from Mexico, we did it for white Texans, not for a bunch of Mexicans.''

''Hear, hear,'' one of the other riders said.

The leader stood in his stirrups and looked out over the band of men who were with him.

''Men of the Texas Liberation Front! We strike for independance! We strike for dignity! We strike for Texas!''

Whooping and shouting, the riders thundered down the

hill. When the caballeros came running from the bunk-houses to see what was going on, they were shot down. Torches were thrown onto the roof of the bunkhouse, the barn, and the main house. Within moments, every building on the ranch was ablaze.

Emile Porter was the publisher, editor, reporter, and type-setter of the *Sweetwater Vindicator*. "We print nothing but the truth," the motto on the newspaper's masthead read.

The *Vindicator* was the third newspaper Emile had started since the end of the war. Both of his earlier papers were still going, but Emile had sold them when he had gotten the urge to move farther west.

Emile was well respected in the town of Sweetwater. He was not only the editor and publisher of the town's only paper, he was also a member of the city council. When his wife had died four years earlier, the entire town had gone into mourning with him. And when he sent his daughter back east to go to college, the town gave her a going-away party that people still talked about.

Emile lifted the tympan, pulled a sheet of paper off the bed, and examined his work.

### NIGHT RIDERS STRIKE AGAIN,
#### Innocent Men Slaughtered

*Last night, a band of masked cowards came out of the dark to burn and murder. Their target was the ranch of Juan Montoya. Their victims were the innocent men who worked for Sr. Montoya. It is said that the riders wanted Montoya to "go back where he came from."*

*What if we all went back to where we came from? What if we all decided to occupy the land that our grandfathers occupied one hundred years ago? If so, Montoya would be the only one left in the county, for he was here long before any of the rest of us.*

*These riders call themselves the Texas Liberation Front. I call them cowards and traitors.*

On the day after Emile's paper appeared, he walked across the street from his newspaper office to have lunch at the City Pig Café. There, as he was nearly every day, he was joined by Phil Weems, the president of the local bank.

"That was quite a good article you wrote about the night riders," Weems said. "Have you gotten any reaction yet?"

"I got a letter to the editor this morning," Emile replied.

"Mail already? That's a very quick response, isn't it?"

"Yes, well, it wasn't exactly a letter to the editor in the traditional sense," Emile said with a laconic smile. "It didn't come in an envelope. It came tied to a rock that was tossed through my window."

"What did it say?"

"It was just your everyday, run-of-the-mill kind of note that's tossed through a window," Emile joked. "Something to the effect that I'm going to be next."

"That's nothing to laugh about, Emile," Weems said.

"No, I guess it isn't," Emile replied. "But I'll be damned if I'll let a bunch of varmints like those cowards who ride around in the dark tell me what I can and what I can't write. As far as I'm concerned, freedom of the press and freedom of speech are special things."

"Well, at least you have the whole town behind you," Weems said.

"I wish that were so," Emile said. "But, amazingly, there are people in this town, and elsewhere, who are actually supporting this nonsensical idea of an independent Texas."

"Well, of course, there are still a few around who can remember when Texas *was* independent," Weems said. "So it isn't exactly like the seed is falling on infertile ground."

The owner of the restaurant came over to their table then.

"Hello, George," Weems asked. "What's good today?"

"The beef stew," George replied. "Phil, I wonder if you

would take a look at this five dollar bill for me." George handed Weems the bill.

Weems had a small magnifying glass in a carrying case in his pocket, and he took it out and used it to examine the bill. After a moment, he looked up. "Where did you get this?" he asked.

"I gave it to him," one of the other customers said. "Why? Is there something wrong with it?"

"It's counterfeit," Weems said. "It's a very good engraving, but it is counterfeit. Where did you get it?"

"I got it in change from the feed store this morning," the customer said.

"What about this bill?" one of the other customers asked, showing Weems a five dollar bill.

Weems took one look at it and shoved it back. "It's counterfeit, I don't even have to look at it."

"How do you know?"

"Same serial number," Weems said. "Did you get it at the feed store, too?"

"No, sir. I got it at your bank," the customer said.

"You got it at the bank?" Weems asked in surprise.

"Yes, sir."

Weems stood up. "Excuse me, Emile, I'd better look into this."

"I'll go with you," Emile said. "If someone is passing counterfeit money around, I should write about it."

Not only Emile, but three or four others from the cafe accompanied Weems as he hurried back to the bank. The tellers and customers looked up in curiosity when they all came tramping in.

"Warren, let me see all the five dollar bills," Weems announced.

"Phil, you think it was only fives?" Emile asked. "Shouldn't you check the other denominations, as well?"

"You're right. Let me see all the fives, tens, and twenties," he said.

"What is it, Mr. Weems?" Warren asked. "What's wrong?"

"I'm just doing some checking, that's all," Weems said.

"Bring all the bills to me, back in my office."

"If we do that, we won't have enough specie to conduct normal business," Warren said.

"For the time being, conduct all business in silver or gold coin only," Weems said.

The customer nearest the teller window caught on to what was going on before anyone else did. He turned to the window. "I want all my money, in coins only, now," he said.

"I want my money in coins as well!" another said, hurrying up to the window.

Groaning, Weems went back to his office as the money was brought to him. Emile went with him.

"Emile, you check the fives, will you? All you have to do is check the serial numbers. If they match, the bills are phoney."

As quietly and as efficiently as they could, Emile and Weems sorted through the paper money. An hour later, they had two stacks—one stack of good money, one stack of bad. Though much more of the money was good than bad, there was a significant amount of bad money.

"Seventeen hundred dollars," Weems moaned, when he counted the bad money.

There was a knock on the door, then one of the tellers opened it and looked inside.

"Mr. Weems, you'd better get out here quick. There's a run on the bank, and we've already run out of silver and gold coins."

"My God," Weems said. "I'm ruined."

"Maybe not, Phil," Emile said. He pointed to the pile of good money. "You've already validated that as genuine. Use it."

"Good idea," Weems said. "Plus, if they see that not all the paper money is bad, it might ease the panic."

Weems stuffed the good money into bags, then started out into the main area of the bank. He was surprised by both the size and the hostility of the crowd he encountered.

"There he is!" someone shouted.

"Weems! We want our money!"

"Yeah! All of it!"

"Warren . . ." Weems began, obviously shaken by what was going on.

"Yes, Mr. Weems?"

"Go down to the telegraph office. Get a wire off to Tom Maxwell in Austin. Tell him to send us fifty thousand dollars as soon as possible."

"I'm not waiting on any money from Austin!" someone shouted. "I want my money now!"

Weems held up the two bags he was carrying. "We've examined the currency in these sacks and there is nothing wrong with it. We'll start paying with it, immediately."

"No paper!"

"You'll get paper money, or you'll get nothing," Weems said, handing the sacks to his tellers. "Start paying," he ordered.

By mid-afternoon the panic had somewhat subsided, because the bank had enough genuine currency on hand to respond to the demand. But the situation was still tenuous and could easily get out of hand if more counterfeit money showed up.

When the Texas Liberation Front held a public rally in Sweetwater that night, the speaker, a man who called himself Colonel Frank Malloy, played upon that fear.

Malloy stood on the back of a wagon. His heavily browed eyes picked up the flickering torchlight and shined as red as if they were reflecting the fires of hell. He was tall and thin, with a full beard and hair that fell to his shoulders. He was wearing a military uniform, though it was not from any recognizable army.

He strode back and forth on the wagon as he talked, his long, bony fingers jabbing into the air to make his points. On the ground in front of him stood his chief of security. The chief of security and the armed men stood with their backs to Malloy, so they could look out over the crowd and guard against any would-be attacker.

"When Texas joined the Union, it joined not as a sub-

49

servient state, carved out of territory already owned by the United States, but as a sovereign nation, equal in authority to the government in Washington. The territory west of Texas was to have been incorporated into Texas.

"But that didn't happen. Instead, the territories of Arizona and New Mexico owe their allegiance to the government in Washington . . . not to the government in Austin. And, what about the Mexican problem? We have Mexicans who are sitting on thousands of acres of good grassland, and good farmland . . . who control water rights to thousands of acres more. And what can we do about them? Nothing, because they are citizens of the United States. Not Texas, mind you. Those of us who live here, and must deal with this problem, have no say whatsoever, because Washington authority supercedes our authority. Is that the way things should be?"

"No!" the crowd replied.

"And now, let me tell you about something else the United States government is doing. You may not have heard of this yet, it may not have reached Sweetwater. But it will, my friends. I have it on very good authority that the United States government is gradually introducing counterfeit money into the economy, here in Texas."

"What? Why . . . it *has* reached here!" someone shouted from the crowd.

"It is already here?" Malloy asked, as if shocked by it.

"Just today, in fact," another from the crowd said. "We near 'bout had a run on the bank."

Malloy put the back of his hand to his forehead, and shook his head slowly. "I didn't know it had reached this far. They are even further along with their plans than I thought."

"What plans?" someone asked.

"Why, can't you see what they are doing? By circulating counterfeit money, they are wreaking havoc with our economy. They want to make every Texan a poor man, because a poor man is a weak man."

"Malloy, that is the biggest bunch of nonsense I have ever heard," Emile said from the back of the crowd.

"And who might you be, sir?" Malloy asked.

"You know who I am. At least, the scoundrels who are with you didn't have any trouble finding my newspaper office this morning."

One of the guards said something and Malloy squatted down to listen to him. They spoke quietly for a moment, then Malloy stood up again.

"Your name is Emile Porter. You own the local newspaper, I believe," Malloy said.

"That's right."

"Well, Mr. Porter, I didn't order anyone to throw a rock through the window, but I can see why someone might want to. I read your article. From what you wrote, one might almost think you want all the Anglos to leave Texas so it can go back to the Mexicans."

"I didn't say anything about a rock being thrown through my window," Emile said.

Malloy coughed in embarrassment, and many in the crowd laughed.

"It is no secret, Mr. Porter. Your paper does not reflect the views of the people. Any one of a hundred men who disagree with you could have thrown that rock."

"No, Malloy. No one in this town did that," Emile replied. "You see, we have had many disagreements over the past several years. Some of the disagreements have been heated. But, in every case, they have been debated in open forum. I have nothing but respect for the man who disagrees with me openly. I have nothing but contempt for the coward who will throw a rock through a window, then run away with his tail between his legs."

Now the crowd, many of whom had been listening attentively to Malloy, applauded Emile. Even those people Emile was talking about, the ones with whom he had disagreed politically, joined in the applause and cheers.

"Go away, Malloy," Emile said. "We don't want you here."

Now the cheers changed to jeers, as the crowd began jeering Malloy.

"You are making a mistake," Malloy said. "All of you!

51

When Texas has regained her independence, you will wish you had joined the movement when you had the chance.''

Malloy nodded at his security officer. The security officer nodded to the four bodyguards, then they went to their horses and formed a mounted screen around the wagon. The wagon driver snapped his reins and the team started ahead. As the wagon and riders disappeared into the darkness at the far end of the street, it was followed by the jeers and catcalls of the citizens of Sweetwater.

# 6

When the telegraph instrument in Jim's private car started to clatter, he looked toward it and saw that the automatic printing machine was spitting out a long ribbon of words. Pouring himself a glass of wine, he waited until the machine was finished, then he went over to retrieve the message he had received.

Although coded messages could be sent and received over the machine, this message was in the clear: "Seventeen hundred dollars in counterfeit money has turned up in Sweetwater, Texas. Counterfeiting in Texas is reaching significant levels. Request you investigate." Jim read it, then reached for the telephone.

The wall-mounted telephone was now a part of the instrumentation in the rather remarkable private car which served not only as Jim and Artemus's headquarters, but also as Jim's personal quarters. The telephone was only good for local communication, and only effective when he was in a city with telephone service. Then, it was merely a matter of becoming a subscriber and connecting his phone to the city line.

As he and Artemus had been doing some investigation for the Denver mint, they had been in the city for a long enough time to make the telephone practical. He cranked the handle.

"Number, please," the operator said.

"Two one seven, operator."

"Thank you."

Jim heard a ring, then someone answered. "Mountain View Hotel."

Artemus was a guest in the Mountain View Hotel, and though he didn't have a telephone in his room, Jim asked that a message be delivered to him requesting that he come over as soon as possible.

Less than half an hour later, Artemus arrived. Jim was standing at the large map of the United States, staring at Texas.

"Why the interest in Texas? Thinking about going into the cattle business?" Artemus teased as he poured himself a glass of wine.

"I was planning our route," Jim said. "We're going to Sweetwater."

"Like they say, see Sweetwater and die," Artie said. "Or is that Salerno?"

"Here it is," Jim said. As Jim began measuring the distance, he nodded toward the message he had received this morning. "Take a look at that."

Sipping his wine, Artie read for a moment, then he looked up. "Jim, have you run this through the classifier yet?"

"Not yet. Why don't we do that and see what we can find?" Jim opened a filing cabinet and pulled out a thick packet of cards.

At first glance, the cards in Jim's hand resembled playing cards. But upon closer inspection it could be seen that, though approximately the same width as playing cards, they were almost twice as long. Also, the cards had a series of holes poked in them, seemingly in random positions.

Jim put the cards into a little box that had been constructed to the exact dimensions to hold them. Next, he connected the box to the top of a hand-crank-operated device that looked a little like the organ-grinder used by musicians who plied the panhandling trade with trained monkeys. Then, putting a lid down over the cards he had just put in the box, he began turning the handle rapidly. Most of the cards shot out from the back of the machine. There, they began stacking up into a receiving box. This box was built to the same dimensions as the feeding box.

Several of the cards, however, were kicked out to the side opposite the crank, where they fell into a third tray. When Jim finished running all the cards through, he picked up the cards that had been ejected to the side. Though not nearly as large as the stack he had started with, there was still a significant number of cards.

"Here are the cities and towns where the phoney money has surfaced," Jim said.

"Change the parameters," Artemus suggested. "Let's run them through again to see what other criminal activity we can find."

Jim made a few adjustments to the machine then ran all the cards through again. When he checked for bank robberies, only two of the cards matched. There were no matches for stage or train holdups. But there was an 86 percent match for arson.

"Well, now," Jim said. "Look at this. Of the twelve towns where counterfeit money has turned up, there have also been incidents of arson."

"Arson?" Artemus replied. "That's a strange combination, don't you think?"

"Yes," Jim said. "I don't know what the connection is . . . but there is a connection."

"Why don't you keep running the cards through the classifier?" Artemus suggested. "And while you are doing that, I'll go make arrangements for a train to move our car."

Two hours later, the *Hesperis*, a trim Baldwin 4-6-0 engine, pulling a seven-car string of varnish, started south on the Denver and Rio Grande line. The seventh car of the string was the private car belonging to Jim West and Artemus Gordon. The two men were sitting in large, overstuffed chairs, watching the countryside roll by. Between them, an open bottle of Cabernet Sauvignon rested in a silver ice bucket.

"Artie, have you ever heard of the Texas Liberation Front?" Jim asked.

"Texas Liberation Front? No, I don't think I have," Artemus replied.

"When the classifier sorted out all the towns for me, I wired the Associated Press office in Houston and got a cross-check on any news items they might have that would pertain to the towns. It seems that in every one of the towns in question, the Texas Liberation Front had held a rally."

"What is the Texas Liberation Front?"

"It is a group of people—rebels, really, who are trying to pull Texas from the union."

Artemus laughed. "Hasn't that issue been settled? Correct me if I'm wrong, but didn't we recently fight a war over that very thing? And Texas was a part of the Confederacy, I believe."

"Yes, but according to the information I received, the Texas Liberation Front is spreading, and one has nothing to do with the other. They are making the claim that Texas alone, of all the states, has the sovereign right to withdraw from the union anytime it wants."

"Is that true?" Aretmus asked.

"It may have been a part of the agreement when Texas was first taken into the union, but if so, I'm sure the Civil War negated it. However, Texas does have a rather unique status among the states. Did you know, for example, that Texas is the only state in the union authorized to fly its state flag at the same height as the national flag?"

Artemus shook his head. "No, I didn't know that."

"That's the kind of information groups like this like to use," Jim said. "They put together truths and half-truths with outright lies, then they come up with something that sounds reasonable."

"Do you think this Texas Liberation Front has anything to do with the counterfeit money?"

"I don't know," Jim admitted. "But I'm sure they are connected with the incidents of arson. There have been no indictments, but, according to the news sources, there have been accusations.''

"Pardon the pun, but where there is smoke, there is usually fire,'' Artemus said.

"Oh, by the way, the cards our classifier kicked out made another interesting little connection,'' Jim said. "Have you ever heard of the Cassias Lear Players?''

"No, I haven't. But it sounds like a theater group.''

"It is,'' Jim said. "A traveling group. Cassias Lear is the owner.''

"That's suspicious enough right there,'' Artemus said.

"Why?''

"Jim, come on, Cassias Lear? Those are two names from Shakespearean drama.''

"You're right. I didn't think about that.''

"I don't know who this Cassias Lear is, but I'd be willing to bet that that isn't his real name. Anyway, what about them?''

"They have also shown up in the same towns.''

"You think it's more than coincidence?'' Artemus asked.

"If so, it is 100 percent coincidence,'' Jim replied. "They have been in every town where counterfeit money has surfaced.''

*Sweetwater, Texas*

It was shortly after midnight, and most of the citizens of Sweetwater were asleep. Two of the town's three saloons were already closed, and though the third was open, it was so dimly lit and had so few customers that it may as well have been closed.

From the west end of town, four riders rode slowly and quietly through the darkness. All four were wearing masks, and two of the four were carrying torches. They rode toward the middle of town, undisturbed and, for the most part, unobserved. They stopped in front of the office of the *Sweetwater Vindicator*.

"Porter!" one of the men called out. "Emile Porter, are you in there?"

There was no answer.

"Porter, we ain't going to give you no more warning! If you're in there, you'd best be comin' out now. We're about to burn that lyin' newspaper of yours down!"

"Ike," one of the men hissed to their leader. "Foster didn't say nothin' 'bout burnin' the buildin'. He just said send 'im a message."

"Yeah, well, Foster ain't here and I am. Besides, fire sends a pretty good message," Ike replied.

A window went up on the second floor and Emile Porter stuck his head out.

"Who are you? What do you want?" Emile called.

"I think you know who we are."

"Yeah, I know who you are," Emile replied. He stuck a shotgun through the window. "You are a bunch of low-life, night-riding cowards. I've got a shotgun here, and I'm pointing it at the four of you. If you don't want your backsides full of shot, you'd better get on out of here."

Covered by the darkness, Ike drew his pistol. Before Emile even knew he was in danger, a shot rang out. Emile dropped the shotgun, then tumbled out of the window, falling heavily onto the dirt street below.

"Jesus! What did you do that for?" one of the men asked. "Nobody said anything about killing him."

"What was I supposed to do, let him shoot us?" Ike replied. "Deke, take a look."

One of the riders dismounted, then went over to look down at Emile's twisted body.

"Is he dead?" Ike asked.

"Yes, he's dead."

"All right, get the broadside nailed up, then set this place afire and let's get out of here."

As one of the men nailed up a poster on a nearby telegraph pole, the others threw their torches through the windows of the newspaper office. Then, even as the citizens of the town began coming out into the street, curious about the gunshot, the four masked men rode away.

The stored paper inside the building caught quickly, and within moments the building was burning fiercely. The wavering light illuminated the poster that the arsonists had left attached to the telegraph pole: "Sic semper tyrannis."

The train, pulling the private railcar of Jim West and Artemus Gordon, arrived before dawn. The two Secret Service agents were asleep when the car was shunted off to a side track, disconnected, and the brakes set.

When Jim awoke the next morning, he pulled the shade to one side and looked out to see where he was. Across the street from the depot, he saw the still-smoking blackened remains of a burned-out building. A dozen or so people were standing out in the street looking on.

Jim got up and dressed, then stepped back to Artemus's room. He rapped on the door.

"Artie, wake up, we're here," he called.

Artemus grumbled something that might have been an answer, and Jim, smiling, left him to awaken at his own convenience.

One of those standing in the street looking at the blackened timbers was wearing a sheriff's badge.

"You Sheriff Mason?" Jim asked.

"I am. Who are you?" Mason replied.

"I'm James West." Jim pointed toward the private railcar that was sitting on the side track. "I arrived early this morning."

"What can I do for you, Mr. West?"

"It's what I can do for you. You sent for me."

"I sent for you?" Mason asked with a puzzled expression on his face.

"Didn't you write a letter to the United States Treasury Department, complaining about counterfeit money?"

"Yes, I did."

"They sent me. I'm with the Secret Service. We deal with such things."

"Is that a fact?" Mason looked over toward Jim's private railcar. "Do all you fellas have private railcars to ride around in?"

"Not all of us," Jim replied. "Tell me about the counterfeit money."

"Oh, yeah, that. Well, whoever is doing it is pretty damn good, I'll tell you. It takes a real expert to tell the difference, and there is so much counterfeit money in circulation that you can hardly get anyone to take paper money anymore," Mason concluded.

"Does this have anything to do with it?" Jim asked, nodding toward the burned building.

"No, I don't think so."

"Accident, then?"

"No, it wasn't that, either," Mason said. "This was the newspaper office. A group of riders came in the middle of the night, killed the editor, and set fire to the building. By the time I woke up and got down here, they were gone, and the building was in flames." Mason pulled a piece of paper from his pocket. "They left this nailed to the telegraph pole," he added, showing it to Jim.

"Sic semper tyrannis," Jim read quietly.

"I beg your pardon?"

"Thus always with tyrants. That is *sic semper tyrannis,* in Latin. It is also the motto of the state of Virginia."

"That's odd," Mason said. "Why would a group of Texas night riders use the motto of the state of Virginia?"

"Then you've seen this before?"

"Oh, yes. They also left it nailed to a tree out on the Montoya place."

"Montoya?"

"Señor Montoya is one of our best Mexican citizens. Hell, he is one of our best citizens, period. But the other night, night riders called on him, burned his house, barn, and all the outbuildings. They killed three of his employees and injured two more."

"Do you know who they were?"

"I suspect they are associated with this so-called Texas Liberation Front," Sheriff Mason replied. "Emile Porter thought that, too. He wrote a big story about it." Mason rubbed his chin. "Hmm, come to think of it, it wouldn't surprise me none if that was why he was killed."

"If you think it's the Texas Liberation Front, why haven't you arrested them?"

"I don't have any real proof," Sheriff Mason said. "The night riders are always masked. The ones you see in the daytime, holding their rallies and such, always obey the law. They say they are being blamed for what the night riders do."

At that moment, at the far end of town, a rider dismounted, pulled a piece of paper from a pouch he was carrying, then began to tack the paper to a wooden fence that connected two buildings.

"Hey! They're back!" someone shouted, pointing to the man.

"Get him!" another in the crowd shouted and, immediately, half a dozen men started running down the street toward the one who was posting the bill.

The bill poster, who was paying attention to the business at hand, didn't notice the group of men running toward him. When he put in the last tack, he stepped back to admire his handiwork. At that precise moment, he was tackled by at least two men.

"What?" he shouted in alarm as he went down.

"String 'im up!" someone yelled. "Bring 'im down here and string 'im up so the whole town can see!"

The man was dragged, kicking and protesting, to the middle of town. When they reached the front of the livery stable, someone threw a rope over a stanchion that protruded from the front.

"Sheriff, aren't you going to do something?" Jim asked.

"If he's one of the men who killed Emile, hanging's too good for him," Mason said with a growl. He sighed. "But I can't let it happen." He started toward the stable to join the others.

"What is this?" the prisoner shouted as he struggled to get free. "Let me go! I haven't done anything!"

Mason held out his hand. "Are there more of those posters in his knapsack?"

"Yes, sheriff. There's a whole bunch of them in here."

"Let me see one of them."

One of the captors pulled out a poster and handed it to Sheriff Mason. Mason looked at it for a moment, then snorted.

"Who are you?" he asked the prisoner.

The prisoner pulled himself up in as dignified a pose as he could, under the circumstances. "Sir," he boomed in a stentorian voice, "my name is T. Linwood Peabody. I am a tragedian."

"You are a what?"

"A tragedian, sir. An actor!"

Mason snorted. "I thought as much." He showed the poster to Jim.

CASSIAS LEAR

begs to announce

the performance by his troupe of players

of the drama

HAMLET

with the great tragedian

CASSIAS LEAR

appearing as

HAMLET

"Let him go," Sheriff Mason said. "He doesn't have anything to do with the Texas Liberation Front. He's an actor."

The men who were holding Peabody prisoner hesitated for a moment.

"You sure about that, sheriff? It wouldn't take much trouble to go ahead and hang him, just to be sure," one of the captors said.

"Let him go," Mason said again.

"You can go on back to join your theater group," Mason said. "The folks will treat you more kindly when you come back."

"Sir, I won't be coming back," Peabody said, resolutely.

"What do you mean, you won't be coming back? Isn't

the theater group coming to Sweetwater?'' Mason asked. He handed Peabody his knapsack.

"It may well come to Sweetwater, sir, but if it does, it will come without me,'' Peabody said. "I have had enough of this godforsaken West. I'm going back East, where people are more civilized.''

Mustering what dignity he had remaining, Peabody threw his knapsack, causing the papers to scatter in the wind. Then he started toward the depot. "I shall be on the next train heading east.''

"What about the horse you rode in on?'' the sheriff called.

"I rented him from the stable the next town over. Turn him loose . . . he'll go back on his own,'' Peabody replied.

# 2

For a small town like Sweetwater, Texas, nothing was as exciting as a traveling theater group. The population was made up of hardworking men and women who had very few diversions. Thus, the posters T. Linwood Peabody left behind in his hasty departure were quickly disseminated by the citizens of the town. By noon, everyone knew that a group of players was arriving, and all began making plans for an evening at the theater.

Here and there, children began putting on impromptu plays, speaking the roles of imaginary characters in loud theatrical voices, then dramatically dying by the sword. Women looked forward to the opportunity to dress up, and even the men commented that they wouldn't mind seeing a "cracking good drama" played out on the stage.

When the train bearing the players arrived at the depot, there were at least three dozen people waiting there, for no other reason than to get a glimpse of the actors.

The three actors who got off the train stood out by the way they were dressed. All three wore three-piece suits, spats, and a cape. The apparent leader of the group also carried a silver-headed cane, and wore a monocle and a Vandyke beard. There was a fourth man with them, a man whose dress and demeanor was more like that of the average person.

"Mr. Lear," this man said, "I have been looking for Mr. Peabody, but he isn't here."

"Don't worry, Mr. Fitzhugh, I'm sure he is around somewhere," Lear replied.

"No doubt we will find him in a bar," one of the actors said.

"Now, now, Mr. Corey, as actors we suffer the slings and arrows of outsiders as it is. There is no need for us to launch missiles at each other," Lear said. "I'm sure Mr. Peabody will turn up shortly, no doubt with a legitimate reason for his absence."

Jim and Artemus were also at the depot watching as the Cassias Lear players detrained. Also detraining, though not a part of the theatrical group, was a young woman dressed in black. Even from here, Jim and Artemus could tell that, had she not been hiding herself with mourning dress, she would be very pretty. She had soft flowing ringlets of chestnut hair, dark blue eyes, and high cheekbones. Two older women were apparently waiting for her, because they greeted her warmly. The three women walked away from the crowd that was welcoming the actors and stood at the far end of the platform, talking quietly. It was obvious that the younger woman was crying, and the two older women were trying to comfort her.

Sheriff Mason was standing nearby, and when he saw Jim looking at the three women, he came closer. "The young woman is Molly Porter," Mason explained.

"Porter? The newspaper publisher?"

"Yes. Molly is his daughter."

"Sad," Artemus said.

"My good fellow," someone called. When Jim and the others looked over, they saw the three actors approaching. "You are the local constabulary, I believe?" the leader of the group asked Mason.

"Constabulary?"

"He's the sheriff," Jim said.

"Yes, that is what I asked."

"What can I do for you?" Mason asked.

"My name, sir, is Cassias Lear. No doubt you have heard of me?" Lear stroked his beard.

"Yes, you are the head of this group of players," Mason said.

"Allow me to introduce my troupe. This is my stage manager, Edward Fitzhugh."

Fitzhugh was about the same size and build as Jim.

"Jason Noble," Lear continued by way of introduction. Noble was a short, rather heavy man. He was bald and clean-shaven.

"And this is Malcolm Corey," Lear concluded. Corey was taller, muscular and also clean-shaven. "There is another member of our troupe, a gentleman by the name of T. Linwood Peabody, who was supposed to meet us here. You wouldn't know anything about him, would you?"

"I'm afraid Mr. Peabody is gone," Sheriff Mason said.

"Gone? What do you mean, gone? Gone where?"

"He said something about going back East."

"Now what do we do, Mr. Lear?" Jason Noble asked. "Miss Fairfield left our troupe last month, Mr. Peabody today. There are only three of us remaining. Hardly enough to stage a performance."

"We will do *Hamlet*," Lear said. "You and Mr. Corey can divide the speaking lines among yourselves, and we will recruit local citizens for nonspeaking parts."

"Perhaps Mr. Fitzhugh could take one of the roles," Corey suggested.

"No, sir," Fitzhugh said, shaking his head. "It would scare me to death to get out on stage."

Lear laughed. "Don't worry, Mr. Fitzhugh, I would not think of thrusting someone before the lights who was not ready for it."

Without another word to Mason, Lear turned and signaled for his troupe to go with him. Moving over to stand in front of the pile of their accompanying equipment, he began outlining how they would mount a performance of *Hamlet* with only the three of them. As the troupe walked away, Jim noticed that the silver-headed cane Lear carried was more than an affectation, for the actor walked with a limp, favoring his left leg.

"They are true artists. In the tradition of the theater, the show must go on," Artemus said.

Jim and Artemus were in the audience that night as the Cassias Lear Players presented *Hamlet*. The play had been surprisingly well done and the audience, who had sat in rapt attention for the entire presentation, now leaned forward in their seats as the final scene was being played out.

Hamlet, portrayed by Lear, drank from a goblet, then let it fall to the stage. The audience, caught up in the drama, was so quiet that the sound of the goblet made many of them jump.

Hamlet staggered to the center of the stage, stopped, turned three-quarters of the way around toward the audience, and put the back of his hand on his forehead.

"O, I die, Horatio; The potent poison quite o'er-crows my spirit: I cannot live to hear the news from England; but I do prophesy the election lights on Fortinbras: he has my dying voice; so tell him, with the occurrents, more and less, which have solicited. The rest is silence."

He gasped, took a couple of staggering steps toward the audience, then pitched forward, falling heavily.

Several in the audience gasped; some of the women began weeping.

Jason Noble, the actor portraying Horatio, moved to stand over Hamlet's body. Placing one hand across his heart, he looked heavenward as he began speaking his lines.

"Now cracks a noble heart. Good night sweet prince: And flights of angels sing thee to thy rest! Why does the drum come hither?"

The role of Prince Fortinbras was played by Malcolm Corey, a third member of the theater group. He came boldly onto the stage.

"Where is this sight?"

Horatio turned to look at him with a snarl on his lips.

"What is it ye would see? If aught of woe or wonder, cease your search."

Prince Fortinbras looked down at the prostrate form of Hamlet.

"This quarry cries on havoc. O proud death, What feast is toward in thine eternal cell, that thou so many princes at a shot o bloodily hast struck?"

The next line should have been spoken by a character in the play called First Ambassador. That role was normally played by T. Linwood Peabody. Peabody's departure had left the theater group a player short, so Malcom Corey also spoke the First Ambassador's line. There were few in the audience who realized the difference.

"The sight is dismal; and our affairs from England come too late: the ears are senseless that should give us hearing, to tell him his commandment is fulfill'd, that Rosencrantz and Guildenstern are dead: where should we have our thanks?"

Noble replied as Horatio: "Not from his mouth, had it the ability of life to thank you: he never gave commandment for their death. But since, so jump upon this bloody question, you from the Polack wars, and you from England, are here arrived give order that these bodies high on a stage be placed to the view; and let me speak to the yet unknowing world how these things came about: so shall you hear of carnal, bloody, and unnatural acts, of accidental judgments, casual slaughters, of deaths put on by cunning and forced cause, and, in this upshot, purposes mistook fall'n on the inventors' reads: all this can I truly deliver."

Fortinbras walked to the front of the stage and lifted his arms.

"Let four captains bear Hamlet, like a soldier, to the stage; for he was likely, had he been put on, to have proved most royally: and, for his passage, the soldiers' music and the rites of war speak loudly for him. Take up the bodies: such a sight as this becomes the field, but here shows much amiss. Go, bid the soldiers shoot."

Four men, dressed in costume but selected from the citizens of the town for this purpose, came out onto the stage.

It was the first theatrical appearance for any of them, and though they had bravely volunteered when the call was made, now they were hesitant and, the moment they stepped into the footlights, they stopped. One of them waved, another put his hand over his eyes and tried to stare over the footlights at the audience. There was a ripple of laughter as the audience saw their own in such unaccustomed roles.

"Go ahead, men," Fitzhugh hissed from the wings. "You know what you are supposed to do."

One of the amateur actors found his courage and started forward. The others went with him and the four reached down to pick up Hamlet. Then, as a drum beat solemnly, they bore him off stage.

As thunderous applause came from the audience, Fitzhugh tugged on the rope to lower the curtain.

"What did you say your name was?" Lear asked. He was in the dressing room of the theater, sitting before a mirror, removing his makeup.

"Wilkes, sir. Horatio Wilkes."

Lear looked around sharply. "You say your name is Wilkes?"

"Yes, sir." Wilkes smiled broadly. "Have you heard of me, sir? My, I didn't know my name would be recognized this far west, but—"

"No. No, I haven't heard of you," Lear said quickly. "I once knew someone named Wilkes, that's all."

"Oh, I see. Well, it is a common enough name back in Georgia. Not that the Wilkeses are common, you understand. I come from a proud old family, which would be wealthy yet today, had it not been for the war and that accursed yankee General Sherman."

Wilkes pulled at the bridge of his nose. "Ah, but I have long since put that unpleasantness behind me. I have been making my living as an actor all these years since, and I would have it no other way."

"What do you want with me, Mr. Wilkes?" Lear asked.

"Why, sir, I would like a position in your troupe,"

Wilkes said. "I could tell by the way you had your actors doubling up on lines tonight that you needed another player."

"You know *Hamlet* well enough to have recognized what we were doing?" Lear asked.

"I am quite familiar with Shakespeare, sir."

"And you wish to audition?"

"I do, sir. I, and one other."

"One other?"

"My niece, sir. Claire Wilkes. She has trained under me and would make an excellent addition for you. Especially as your troupe is noticeably absent of female players."

"Where is your niece now?"

"She is waiting just outside the door, sir. I did not wish to presume," Wilkes said.

Lear stood up from the dressing table. "All right, we have a matinee tomorrow. Before the curtain rises, you and your niece can audition. Make arrangements with Mr. Fitzhugh, our stage manager."

"What? You mean we are to audition before an audience?" Wilkes sputtered. "But . . . I've never heard of such a thing . . . auditioning before an audience. What would you have us do?"

"Do? Do anything you want to do," Lear said. "You are the one who came to mé with the request to audition."

Wilkes nodded. "Very well, sir. We will come up with something," he said.

Although it was announced that the Cassias Lear Players would be doing another performance of *Hamlet,* the theater was as full for the matinee as it had been the night before. Indeed, many in the audience had been here for the previous performance.

Edward Fitzhugh, the stage manager, was standing in the stage wings. A small podium was in front of him, and on the podium was a tablet with stage directions and production instructions. As each task was accomplished, Fitzhugh would mark it off. He looked over at Wilkes and nodded. "All right, you folks are on," he said.

Wilkes and the young woman were standing in the wings a few minutes before show time.

"I'm very nervous. I don't know if I can do this," the young woman said.

"My dear, as beautiful as you look, you could merely stand on the stage and succeed," Wilkes said.

The young woman smiled nervously, then touched her hair, which was now blond, and pulled at the daringly low scoop at the neckline of her dress. There was a dramatic application of blue eye shadow, which had the effect of making her eyes look green.

"I'll be all right," the girl said. "I just wanted to be reassured, one more time, that I can do this."

"Trust me, you'll do fine," Wilkes said.

"Are you ready, Mr. Wilkes?" Lear asked, coming over to join them.

"Quite ready, sir."

"Remember, I want them in the proper mood when the curtain goes up."

"I'll see what I can do," Wilkes said.

Wilkes walked out onto the stage, tipped his hat forward, leaned on his cane like a dandy, and began his recitation:

"I came home the other night,
    as drunk as I could be.
And what do you think my wondering
    eyes should see?
A horse, where my horse should be.
So I said to my wife, my pretty little wife,
'Explain this thing to me.
What's a horse doing, where my horse should be?'
And she said, 'You old fool, you drunken old fool,
    can't you plainly see?
That's nothing but a milk cow
    my mama gave to me.' "

The audience roared with appreciative laughter, and Wilkes went on.

"Well, I've been around this country
    maybe ten times or more.
But a saddle and bridle on a milk cow,
I never saw before."

More laughter.

"I came home the other night,
    as drunk as I could be.
And what do you think my wondering
    eyes should see?
A hat, hanging on the hat rack,
    where my hat ought to be.
So, I said to my wife, my pretty little wife,
'Explain this thing to me.
What's this hat doing on the hat rack,
    where my hat ought to be?'
And she said, 'You old fool, you drunken fool,
    can't you plainly see?
That's nothing but a chamber pot
    my mama gave to me.'
Well, I've been around this country,
    maybe ten times or more.
But a feather on a chamber pot,
I never saw before."

"What happened next?" one of the men in the audience
yelled.
"You didn't believe that, did you?" another asked.
Wilkes, playing the injured and innocent husband, tipped
his hat back and stepped forward as if taking the audience
in on his story.

"I came home the other night,
    as drunk as I could be.
And what do you think my wondering
    eyes should see?"

"With you, there's no tellin!" one of the men shouted,
and all guffawed with laughter. Wilkes, playing the crowd

72

beautifully, merely raised one eyebrow as if totally taken in by it all, then he continued.

"I saw pants, on a chair,
   where my pants ought to be."

"Mister, you had better wake up," someone shouted.

"So, I said to my wife, my pretty little wife,
'Explain this thing to me.
What are these pants doing here,
where my pants ought to be?' "

"I'd like to hear her get out of that!" someone yelled.

"And she said, 'You old fool, you drunken fool,
   can't you plainly see?
That's nothing but a dishrag
   my mama sent to me.'
Now, I've been around this country,
   maybe ten times or more.
But belt and buttons on a dishrag,
I never saw before."

"Why, you old fool, don't you know what that woman's doing to you?" someone in the front row yelled.

"I came home the other night,
   as drunk as I could be.
And what do you think my wondering
   eyes should see?
A head, on the pillow,
Where my had should be."

"I told you!" one of the men shouted. "You should'a figured that woman out the moment you saw that strange horse."

Wilkes raised his hand and pointed his finger. He made

a face like an irate husband challenging his wife with ir-refutable evidence.

> "So I said to my wife, my pretty little wife,
> 'Explain this thing to me.
> What is this head doing on my pillow,
>    where my head ought to be.'
> And she said, 'You old fool, you drunken fool,
>    can't you plainly see?
> That's nothing but a mushmelon
>    my mama sent to me.' "

"A mushmelon?" one of the men in the audience shouted. "And you believed her?"

> "Well, I've been around this country
>    maybe ten times or more.
> But a mustache on a mushmelon,
> I never saw before.
> Yes, a mustache on a mushmelon,
> I never saw before."

Wilkes finished his recitation with a sweeping bow, then left the stage to the howls of laughter from an appreciative audience.

Fitzhugh, Noble, and Corey were all three laughing when Wilkes left the stage, but Lear was scowling.

"Mr. Wilkes, it cannot have escaped your notice that we are doing *Hamlet* tonight," Lear growled. "*Hamlet*! You do understand, don't you, that it is a tragedy, and not a comedy? You have the entire audience laughing like fools."

"He has them laughing because he did a very good job with his recitation," Fitzhugh said.

"Mr. Fitzhugh, as you are a stage manager, and not an actor, I don't expect you to understand," Lear said. "I would appreciate it if you would just do your job and make no references to mine."

"Yes, sir," Fitzhugh said contritely.

"Mr. Lear, I understand what you are saying," Wilkes said. "But not to worry. My niece has a dramatic recitation that will get them back in the mood for *Hamlet*."

Wilkes looked over at Claire, then nodded. "Go ahead, my dear," he invited.

Claire took a deep breath, then walked out onto the stage. She stood there for a long moment as the residual laughter from Wilkes's presentation died.

"What is she doing?" Lear asked. "Why doesn't she say something?"

"Because she knows how to play the crowd," Wilkes replied. "Surely sir, a great and respected tragedian such as yourself recognizes that."

"Yes, of course," Lear said. "I can understand that, perfectly. But I didn't know that she did, and I thought that perhaps she was suffering from stage fright."

"No, she is fine," Wilkes said. He held up his finger. "Shh, she's about to begin."

Clear and sweet, Claire's voice rolled out over the audience.

"We marched across the stormy land
With strong and fearless tread,
Though worn with toils scantily
Supplied with wartime bread.
No stimulant but blood that burned
Our suffering race to save,
Following with joy our youthful chief
To victory or the grave.
Sulphurous flames from countless guns
Illume the grim night air,
No fitful flash, but blazes on
With one continuous glare!
We staggered not . . . we halted not
For wounded friend or dead.
Through surging shell and hissing shot
Fast toward the foe we sped.
'Onward, my boys!' our leader's voice

Rings cheerily o'er the storm,
'We'll gain the parpet, and there
Your shattered ranks reform.
Onward my friends, my heroes, come,
For every human right.
For kindred, country, hearth, and home,
Honor and freedom fight.' "

Claire left the stage to a thunderous applause, for there were many in the audience who, sixteen years earlier, had fought in the war, and her words resonated deep within their hearts. More than one man with gray beginning to fleck his hair turned aside to wipe away tears that they thought no one else saw.

"Now, Mr. Lear," Wilkes said as Claire came off the stage, "you may give them *Hamlet*."

# 8

"Then you are . . ."

"I am Christina, the one called the Midnight Angel," Claire answered.

"We owe much to you," Wilkes said, speaking the role of Dr. Bernard.

"Then I take back any unkind thought I may have had about this woman," Cassias Lear said, in the role of Count DuMont. "Will that make things right?"

"No," the Midnight Angel replied. "Not until I have made a name for myself, won something from fame which fortune has denied me."

"What proud words!" Dr. Bernard exclaimed.

"Worthy words . . . from . . . ," Count DuMont turned to face the audience as he mouthed the last of his line, to make certain that they heard the dramatic conclusion: "the Midnight Angel."

Claire thrust her arms upward, as if in appeal to the heavens, and every other member of the troupe assumed a rigid pose in a grand tableau as the curtain descended to thunderous applause.

"Bravo!" the audience yelled. "Bravo, bravo, bravo!"

"Hold the tableau," Lear hissed. "The curtain is coming back up."

The curtain lifted again and the players were still in the same position, holding rigid expressions on their faces, making what Cassias Lear liked to call a living portrait. This was his specialty, and he was very proud of his tableau curtain calls.

The applause grew louder and the audience rose from their seats as they continued to cheer. The curtain descended one more time, and this time the players broke the tableau and prepared for their final bows. The curtain rose again, and one by one the actors stepped forward to receive their due.

A long-stemmed rose was tossed to Claire, and her eyes sparkled brightly as she held it to her nose, smiling at the audience as the curtain descended for the final time.

"Mr. Wilkes, you were wonderful," Fitzhugh said. "Mr. Lear, don't you think he is a wonderful replacement for T. Linwood Peabody? In fact, he is all the more valuable because he brought his talented niece with him. They were both wonderful."

"I thought he and his niece were adequate," Lear said.

"Merely adequate, sir?" Wilkes asked, looking at him questioningly. "I don't mind your demeaning my poor efforts, but you must admit that my niece is a young woman of remarkable talent."

"Please, sir, don't be insulted at my suggestion that you and your niece were merely adequate. What I consider adequate, most others would consider superb," Lear said. "It is just that I, as I am sure the others will bear witness, have a most exacting standard. However, I no longer consider you and your niece on probation. You have a permanent position in my troupe, should you desire to take it."

"Yes, we do want it. Thank you."

"I am curious, though. You are about my age, and obviously experienced. You must've had a long stage career. And yet, I have never heard of you."

"I have done nearly all of my work back East," Wilkes answered. "It is only recently that I got the urge to travel West."

"Just because you are in the West, Mr. Wilkes, never

believe for one moment that our audiences aren't devotees of the theater. You will find them every bit as cosmopolitan as the audiences of Boston, New York, Philadelphia, and Washington.''

"Oh, have you played in our nation's capital?" Wilkes asked.

"Yes," Lear replied. "In fact, some years ago I gave the best performance of my life there." He stared at Wilkes for a long moment, as if deep in thought, then he came out of his reverie and looked around at the others. "Pack your things, people. We have another town to play.''

The Cassias Lear players were waiting for the next train east. The actors had a sense of the dramatic about them. Even in private conversations their voices projected, as if they were on stage. They rolled their r's, and broadened their vowels, and their very existence was a performance.

Wilkes sat with them for a few moments, then got up and started to walk away.

"Where are you going?" Fitzhugh asked.

"Nowhere in particular," Wilkes answered. "I'm just going to stretch my legs a bit.''

"Please don't miss the train," Fitzhugh said. "Mr. Lear would be very upset, and I'm afraid he would hold me responsible.''

Wilkes smiled. "Don't you worry about that, Mr. Fitzhugh. I shall be back in plenty of time to catch the train.''

Fitzhugh nodded, then sat on a bench near the depot and looked out toward the track. He had done his part to ensure that Wilkes was present when the train departed. That was all he could do.

Wilkes made a big show of stretching, then he started walking. When he got to the edge of the building, he stepped around the corner. This was where the telegraph wires came into the depot. Looking around to make certain no one was watching him, Wilkes pulled a small telegraph key from his pocket. He connected it to the telegraph wires, and began tapping out a message.

•   •   •

The telegraph began clacking in Jim's private railcar. Jim walked over to it and watched as the narrow little strip of paper began unwinding. The message read: "Molly and I have been totally accepted as members of the troupe. You were right to recruit her. She is a fine actress and will, no doubt, be of great help to us. Use the classifier to see what you can find out about Cassias Lear, Jason Noble, Malcolm Corey, and Edward Fitzhugh."

Jim smiled. He hadn't had the slightest doubt that as Horatio Wilkes, Artemus would be able to secure a position as an actor with the Cassias Lear Players. He had worried about Molly Porter portraying Artemus's niece, though.

He needn't have worried. As Artemus discovered, Emile Porter's daughter was a natural. She had participated in many theatricals while in finishing school, so appearing on stage was not difficult for her. And having some hand in bringing to justice her father's killers certainly provided her with all the motivation she needed. She didn't have to worry about being identified, either. Artemus was such a genius with makeup that by the time he finished with her no one in town could recognize her.

In fact, to prove his point, and to give Molly confidence in the makeover job he had done with her, Artemus took her to church, where he introduced her as his niece. Not even the two women who had met her at the depot when she came back to town recognized her.

Jim went over to the classifier, opened the drawers, and pulled out several of the punched cards. He fed them into the chute, then started turning the crank.

When all the card runs were finished, he made a file of the information he had gathered.

Name: Cassias Lear
Age: 43 years; Height: 5 feet 7 inches
Weight: 145 pounds; Build: slender
Complexion: dark
Color of hair: dark
Color of eyes: brown
Wears Vandyke beard, well trimmed

Occupation: actor
No known criminal record

Name: Jason Noble, also known as Sidney Moffet
Age: 37 years; Height: 5 feet 6 inches
Weight: 165 pounds; Build: rotund
Complexion: light
Color of hair: chestnut, balding
Color of eyes: blue; Clean-shaven
Occupation: actor, scam artist, petty thief
There are no federal warrants for Jason Noble, but he
served two years in the federal prison at Leavenworth,
Kansas for passing counterfeit money.

Name: Malcolm Corey, no known aliases
Age: 34 years; Height: 5 feet 11 inches
Weight: 175 pounds; Build: muscular
Complexion: swarthy
Color of hair: flaxen
Color of eyes: blue; Clean-shaven
Occupation: actor, gambler, bouncer
Held up stagecoach in Wyoming, sentenced to five
years, served time. No federal warrants.

Name: Edward Fitzhugh
(No Information Available)

It was interesting, Jim thought, that two of the four members of the Cassias Lear Players had criminal records. It
was particularly interesting that one of them had a history
of dealing in counterfeit money. He was also curious about
Edward Fitzhugh. It seemed very unlikely that a person
could be as invisible as Fitzhugh seemed to be. There had
to be some record of him somewhere. And yet, there apparently was nothing on him.

Jim made notes for Artemus, though he had no idea how
he was going to pass the information along to his friend
and partner.

In the meantime, Jim had his own work to do. He had

gotten word that some counterfeit money had turned up in the town of Phantom Hill, so he decided to go over and have a look around. As it was some distance away from the nearest railroad, he left the car in Sweetwater and proceeded on horseback.

He had been on the road for about an hour when he heard gunshots. Urging his horse into a gallop, he raced to the top of the next hill. No more than a quarter of a mile in front of him, he saw an elegant coach, moving quickly down the road, its wheels throwing up rooster plumes of dust which hung in little clouds over the road behind it.

Four men on horseback were chasing the coach. All the gunfire was coming from those on horseback, and nobody on the coach was firing back. The coach seemed to be doing nothing more than trying to get away from them.

Jim could see that the road would soon make a bend around the far end of the same ridge he was now on. He started along the top of the ridge, then sloped his horse down toward the road on the other side. He reached the road just as the coach rounded the bend and, for a moment, he saw fear in the driver's eyes. The driver started to stop the coach.

"No!" Jim shouted. "Keep going! I'm here to help you!"

Nodding, the driver urged his team on. Jim fell in alongside the coach, then, turning in his saddle, began firing at the four men who were in pursuit. His first shot dropped one of the riders. His second shot wounded one of the others and, seeing that they were no longer unopposed, the riders stopped, then turned their horses and rode away.

"They're going away!" Jim shouted. "You'd better slow your team now, or you're going to kill them."

"*Si, señor!*" the driver said, pulling the team first to a walk, then, after a few moments, stopping them.

As canvas curtains were hanging over the windows, Jim couldn't see inside the coach.

"Is anyone inside?" Jim asked.

One of the curtains was pulled aside, and an old Mexican woman looked outside.

"Are you going to hurt us, señor?" the woman asked.

The driver said something in Spanish, and the old woman smiled. *"Gracias, señor."* She said something to someone who was inside the coach and, a moment later, the coach door opened and a beautiful young Mexican woman stepped down.

"Juan says you saved our lives," the woman said in accentless English. "I thank you, sir."

"Who were those men?" Jim asked.

"They call themselves the Texas Liberation Front," the driver said. He spat in disgust.

"Why would the Texas Liberation Front be after you?"

"I am Carmelita Gonzales," the girl said. "My brother is Ricardo Gonzales. Do you know him?"

"No, I'm afraid not," Jim said. "I'm not from around here."

"Then perhaps you do not know that men who call themselves the Texas Liberation Front have been conducting a campaign of evil. They have killed our people, burned our homes, and stolen our animals. Most are poor and cannot defend themselves, but my brother is a very wealthy man and he has fought back. I think, perhaps, they wanted to capture me as a means of getting to my brother."

"I think you might be right," Jim said. "How far is it to your ranch?"

"About one more hour," Carmelita replied.

Jim tied his horse onto the coach, then pulled his rifle from the saddle sheath. "Juan, do you have room for someone to ride up there with you?"

*"Si, señor!"* Juan said with a happy smile.

"Then, why don't I just go with you to see that you get back all right?" Jim suggested.

"My brother will reward you handsomely," Carmelita said.

Jim smiled. "Señorita Gonzales, we should reach your house at just about dinnertime," he said. "I would think an invitation to dinner would be reward enough."

• • •

83

Rancho del Rey was one of the most attractive ranches Jim had ever seen. The stucco hacienda had castellated walls and a red-tile roof. It consisted of a main structure and two wings. The wings were at forty-five degree angles to the main structure, thus creating a courtyard. The courtyard was beautifully landscaped, making use of red and green tiles, a pond, and flower beds of every hue and variety. Two gardeners were at work as the coach drew to a stop in front of the house.

Even before the coach arrived, it had been spotted by one of Gonzales's men. Seeing that an Anglo was riding on the seat with the driver, he thought it unusual enough to report. As a result of his report, the *patron* himself had come out to greet the coach. There was a worried expression on his face until the door to the coach opened and Carmelita stepped out.

Gonzales grinned broadly at the sight of his sister and he opened his arms for an embrace.

"Ricardo, some men attacked us," Carmelita said. "But this gentleman drove them off. Señor Jim West, this is my brother, Don Ricardo Gonzales."

"I am honored, Don Gonzales," Jim said, extending his hand.

"No, señor, the honor is mine. How can I repay you?" He laughed. "That is a foolish question. My sister's safety is beyond price. But I will try."

"Ricardo, he has asked only to have dinner with us," Carmelita said.

"Dinner? But of course, dinner, lodging, anything you want, señor. Ask, and it is yours."

"I do have a few questions I would like to ask," Jim said, "about the Texas Liberation Front."

The smile left Gonzales's face, and his eyes narrowed.

"They are evil men, señor," he said. "Why do you wish to know about them?"

"Because I want to put them out of business," Jim replied. "Don Gonzales, I am an agent for the United States Secret Service. These people represent a threat against the United States and its citizens." Jim took in the ranch with a wave of his arm. "And by its citizens I mean you and your people. It would seem that the Texas Liberation Front has a particular vendetta against Mexican-Americans."

"That is true," Gonzales said. "I do not think they can hurt me, here. I am too strong for them. But the poor . . . ah, señor, they can hurt the poor very much." Gonzales smiled. "But we can discuss that later, after dinner."

After a dinner in which the food never seemed to stop coming, Jim was invited into a large room where he was offered wine and a cigar.

"May I light the cigar for you, señor?" Carmelita asked, bending over him.

When Jim looked up toward her, he saw that she had removed her jacket. The result was a delightful view of her breasts. He took them in with a long, unabashed look, then raised his eyes to meet hers. She held his gaze, as if letting him know that she not only knew what he had been looking at, but that she would have been disappointed if he had not availed himself of the opportunity she had presented.

Ricardo Gonzales cleared his throat, and Carmelita struck the match, let the sulphur flare away, then held the flame to the tip of Jim's cigar.

"Thank you very much," Jim said.

"You are welcome," Carmelita said.

"Carmelita, play some music for our guest."

"Perhaps Señor West doesn't like music," Carmelita suggested.

"No," Jim said. "I love music." He looked around the room. "There's no piano in here. Shall we go to another room?"

Carmelita laughed. "I play the guitar, señor."

"Are you familiar with the guitar, señor?" Ricardo Gonzales asked.

"Yes, of course."

"Señor, I know you have heard the guitar used to accompany those who would sing. But I meant, are you familiar with it as a concert instrument? It was invented by the Spanish, you know, and we didn't invent it to sing songs to the cows as do the Anglos.''

"I hope I do not disappoint you," Carmelita said as she picked up a guitar. "This was my grandfather's guitar," she said. "It is very old."

The box was cherry red, giving way to a soft yellow. It showed tender care, and the way Carmelita handled it, gently, and with respect, told the story of her love for the instrument. She strummed the strings lightly, moving through an intricate chord progression that rose from the sound box and wove a pattern of melody as delicate as a lace doily.

Jim sat quietly, listening in delight.

Carmelita went through the chord progressions a few times, and then stopped. She hung her head for a few seconds, then started to play. The music spilled out—a steady, never-wavering beat with two or three poignant minor chords at the ends of phrases, but with an overall, single string melody, weaving in and out of the chords like a thread of gold woven through the finest cloth.

The sound was agony and ecstasy, joy and sorrow, pain and pleasure. Jim felt himself being carried along with the melody, now rising, now falling. It was nothing he had ever heard before, and yet it had an aching familiarity to it. It was the music of a proud people, a people who found themselves thrust into a culture totally foreign to their own, for reasons beyond their control.

When the echo of the last note died away, Jim applauded.

"Beautiful," he said.

"It is too bad that Miguel isn't here," Gonzales said. "If he were here to play the instrument, my sister could dance for us."

*"Permiso,"* Jim said, holding out his hand toward the guitar.

With a look of curiosity and surprise, Carmelita handed the instrument to him.

To the delight of everyone present, Jim began playing the guitar, not in the cording way of "singing to the cows," as Gonzales had talked of, but in the same Spanish style as

86

Carmelita. But whereas hers was an intricate weaving of melody and minor chords, Jim was playing with an aggressive, moving beat, augmented by slapping his hand against the box itself.

Smiling at him, Carmelita moved out to the center of the room and, lifting her arms over her head, began to dance. She clapped her hands, tossed her hair, swivelled her hips, and stomped the floor as she danced to the music. And as she danced, her bright, yellow dress swirled out, showing a pair of long, shapely legs.

Taking his cue from her, Jim continued to play until he was certain she had completed her dance. Then, with a thunderous crescendo of foot stomping, she brought the dance to a close.

"Bravo! Bravo, Señor West, bravo Carmelita!" Gonzales said, applauding enthusiastically.

Suddenly one of Gonzales's men came bursting into the room.

"Don Gonzales!"

"Señor Gomez, what is it?" Gonzales asked. "What brings you in here in such a state?"

"*Mal hombres,* Don Gonzales. They come."

Gonzales looked at Jim. "The evil ones you asked about are here," he said. "I am surprised; I did not think they would attack me here."

"Are you ready for them?" Jim asked.

"*Si.* If they want war, we can give them war."

Gonzales ordered the women to go to a safe place, then he and Jim hurried outside.

# 9

Colonel Frank Malloy of the Texas Liberation Front held up his hand, and the men who were riding with him stopped.

"Ike, get up here," he called.

Ike Jacobson, a big man with a handlebar mustache, moved up beside Malloy.

"There's the ranch."

"Look at the size of it," Ike said. "That's even bigger than the Montoya place. Can you imagine a Mexican being rich enough to own something like that?"

"Yeah, well, after we take Texas back, none of 'em will," Malloy said. "You know what to do?"

"Same thing we did to Montoya, right? Kill as many as we can, burn what we can."

"No, don't burn anything."

"Don't burn anything?" Ike asked in surprise.

Malloy smiled. "I plan to own this place someday," he said. "Why would I want to burn it?"

Ike laughed. "Yeah, good point. I didn't think of that."

"Get 'em started," Malloy said.

Nodding, Ike rode back to the others. "All right, men," he said. "Shoot as much as you want, kill anything that moves, but don't burn the place," he ordered.

He pulled his pistol and held it over his head, signaling for the others to do the same thing. When everyone had drawn their guns, he nodded, then turned, and led them toward the sprawling ranch.

"How long before they get here?" Jim asked.

"Gomez spotted them on the east rim, so it shouldn't be long," Gonzales replied. "Maybe five minutes." Gonzales began shouting to his men, and Jim saw that he was sending half of them to a stone fence on the left side of the approach, while directing the other half toward a ditch on the right.

"Don Gonzales, wait," Jim said. "It is good that you have divided your men to catch them in a cross fire, but some should remain here to draw them in."

"*Si, señor,* you are right," Gonzales said, and he altered his orders so that a few of the men stayed back.

As Jim studied the layout, he saw a barn that overlooked the approach to the house.

"I am going to the barn," Jim called back over his shoulder as he started toward it. From the loft of the barn, he would have a clear shot at any of the approaching riders.

By the time Jim reached the barn, he saw that all the others were in position as well. Gonzales and two of his men were in the middle. Their job was simple. They would draw the attackers into the ambush.

The riders approached.

Jim waited until the riders were well within range.

*"Now!"* Jim shouted as loudly as he could. He stood up, raised his rifle to his shoulder and fired.

With a surprised grunt of pain, one of the approaching riders fell from his saddle.

"What the . . . !" Ike shouted. "Carl, where did that come from?"

"I don't know!" the rider named Carl answered.

At that moment, the men who were hidden behind the stone wall and in the ditch rose up and began firing. The effect was devastating, as at least three more men went down.

A moment earlier, the men who called themselves the Texas Liberation Front had thought they were riding in to attack an easy target. But in less than a second, their operation had gone from one of quiet confidence to one of barely controlled terror. Frightened and surprised by the sudden and unexpected ambush, they tried to get control of their bolting horses.

"Ike, they got Leroy and Parker!" Carl shouted. Getting his horse under control, he jerked it around and dug his spurs into the animal's flanks. Just as he did so, a bullet crashed into the back of his head.

"Carl!" one of the others shouted, but his next word was cut off as a bullet entered his own back, tore through his heart, and exited through his chest.

For fully sixty seconds, guns roared and bullets whined.

"Let's get out of here!" someone shouted, and when he turned to ride away, those who were still mounted turned to ride away with him.

"No! Come back here and fight, you cowards!" Ike called.

When he saw that his entreaties toward them would have no effect, Ike realized that he would have no choice but to join them. Thinking to avoid the bullets, Ike swerved his horse toward the barn. That was when he saw someone standing on the ground in front of the barn door. Because the person on the ground wasn't Mexican, Ike thought at first that it was one of his men. When he got closer, though, he realized that it wasn't. Startled, he pulled his horse to a stop.

"Who are you?" he asked.

"My name is James T. West," Jim said. "I am an agent for the Secret Service, and you are under arrest."

"Arrest?" Ike scoffed. "Get out of my way, mister. I don't have time for the likes of you."

In a sudden, and unexpected move, Jim tossed a loop around Ike.

"Get this off me, you fool!" Ike growled. He reached up to slide the loop off.

Jim raised his hand and pointed it toward the open window of the hayloft, the position from which he had begun the firing. There was a flash of light and a puff of smoke as, from his sleeve, a sharp-pointed bolt was suddenly propelled upward. The bolt slammed into the wall beside the window. At almost the same moment, a spring-activated device caused the rope to begin to wind up. That had the effect of pulling Ike from his saddle and drawing him up into the air.

"Hey!" Ike shouted, frightened and surprised at what was happening to him. "What's going on here?"

Ike was now suspended from the top of the barn. His gun lay on the ground below him while his horse, confused by the sudden absence of his rider, dashed away. In the distance, too far away to provide any assistance, Ike saw his men riding away—that is, those who could ride. Five of them were lying on the ground whey they had fallen.

Now the final gunshot was rolling back, no more than an echo as Gonzales and the others stood up cautiously.

Holding smoking guns at the ready, the defenders walked slowly toward the twisted forms that were lying on the ground. None was moving, and all five were silent.

"Are they all dead?" Gonzales asked.

"*Si, señor,*" Gomez answered.

"Get me down from here!" Ike shouted. He was still dangling from the top of the barn, like a fish on a hook.

When Gonzales and the others saw him, they began to laugh.

"It ain't funny, dammit!" Ike called. "Get me down!"

Jim raised his pistol and pointed it at Ike.

"No, for God's sake, don't shoot me!" Ike pleaded.

When Jim fired, his bullet severed the cord by which Ike was suspended, and he fell. Ike hit the ground, then pitched forward, landing facedown in a pile of manure. Again, Gonzales and his men laughed at him.

"What do we do with him?" one of Gonzales's men asked, pointing at Ike.

Gomez pulled a dagger and put the point to Ike's neck. "I will take care of him," he said. Ike cringed in fear.

"No!" Jim said quickly. "Put the knife away."

"Señor, he does not deserve to live," Gomez replied.

"I said put the knife away," Jim said. "I have put him under arrest. He is my prisoner, and I need him."

Gomez looked at Gonzales, who nodded. With a sigh of disappointment, Gomez put his knife away, then stepped back.

"You are a lucky man, señor," Gomez said to Ike. "This Anglo has saved your life."

"Don Gonzales! Don Gonzales, come quick!" someone shouted from the house. "Your sister! She is gone!"

Gonzales started toward the house on the run, with Jim right beside him. When they got inside, they found the maid crying. Her eye was blackened and her lip bruised.

"Maria, what happened?" Gonzales asked.

"Anglos took her," Maria said. "While you were fighting in front, they come in the back. I try to fight them off but they beat me, here." She pointed to her face. "And then they took Donna Carmelita with them."

"I am going after them," Gonzales said.

"Don Gonzales, no, you mustn't go!" Jim said, holding his hand out as if to stop him.

"Señor, they have taken my only sister. Do you think I will do nothing?"

"If you go after her, you will be doing exactly what they want you to do. Don't you see? They are trying to draw you away from the ranch. If you leave it now, you may have nothing left when you return."

"If harm comes to my sister and I did nothing to help her, I will never forgive myself," Gonzales said.

"If they wanted to harm Carmelita, they wouldn't have taken her with them. They would have killed her here, when they had the chance."

At that moment, Gomez brought Ike over.

"Here is your prisoner, señor."

"What's your name?" Jim asked the prisoner.

"I ain't tellin' you nothin'."

Jim put his hand onto Ike's chin, and forced his mouth open. "You know, you have a bad tooth there," he said. "You really should do something about it."

"What?" Ike asked, confused by the strange comment. "What do you care about my teeth?"

"Señor Gonzales, do you have anyone who is good at dentistry? Someone who could pull a tooth?"

"Yes," Gonzales said. He nodded toward his foreman. "Gomez has pulled many teeth."

Jim looked at Gomez. "Señor Gomez, I would like you to pull one of his teeth."

"*Si, señor,*" Gomez replied. "Which one?"

"It doesn't matter, pull any one you want. They all offend me."

"What? Are you crazy?" Ike demanded.

"Then I'll ask you again. What is your name?" Jim asked.

"Jacobson. Ike Jacobson," Ike answered.

"Who took the girl, Jacobson?"

"Colonel Malloy took her," Ike said.

"And who is Colonel Malloy?"

Ike looked at Jim in surprise. "Frank Malloy. *The* Frank Malloy! Don't tell me you've never heard of him?"

"I've never heard of him," Jim replied. "Who is he?"

"He's the military head of the Texas Liberation Front, that's who he is. That makes him one of the most important men in Texas."

"I see," Jim replied. "And why would one of the most important men in Texas, the military head of the Texas Liberation Front, want to take an innocent young woman as his prisoner?"

"He said if we had her it would give us a bargaining position," Ike said.

"What sort of bargaining position?"

"I . . . I don't know," Ike replied. "I'm not smart enough to understand stuff like that. That was just something Colonel Malloy said."

"Where is Malloy taking her?"

Ike's dark, beady eyes began darting around the room. He looked like a cornered rat. "I don't know where he is taking her," he mumbled.

"Ike, I believe you are lying," Jim said.

"I've already told you all I'm goin' to tell you," Ike said.

"Señor Gomez, start pulling teeth," Jim said.

"No, no! Look, I really don't know where he is taking her."

"I don't believe you," Jim said. "Señor Gomez?"

Gomez, who was now armed with a pair of pliers, started toward Ike.

"No, no! Wait!" Ike shouted. "Look, all I know is he said he would meet us at Truby."

"Truby?"

"Truby is northeast of here," Gonzales said. "One hundred and fifty miles. It is a . . . how do you say? *Población de espectro.*"

"Town of ghosts?" Jim asked. Then he smiled. "You mean, it is a ghost town?"

"*Sí, sí,* a ghost town."

"Then I'll find it. And I'll find her," Jim said.

"What about this man, señor?" Gomez asked. "Do you leave him with us?"

Jim looked at Ike. "Take him into town, Gomez. Tell the sheriff to hold him in jail for me until I get back."

Ike laughed. "You are having a Mex take me into town? Do you really think the sheriff is going to put a Texan in jail on the word of a Mexican?"

"He is right, señor," Gomez said. "I do not believe the sheriff will put a gringo in jail on the word of a Mexican."

Ike smiled. "Now what are you going to do, mister?" he asked Jim.

Jim shrugged. "If the sheriff won't put him in jail, kill him."

"What?" Ike gasped.

"Very good, señor," Gomez said, smiling broadly.

"What?" Ike gasped. "Are you crazy? You can't do that!"

"Oh, I can do pretty much anything I want," Jim said. "So when I come back, you will either be in jail, or you will be dead. If I were you, I would help these gentlemen convince the sheriff that you should be in jail."

• • •

As she rode away from her brother's ranch, Carmelita was working on part of her dress, rubbing it against a rough corner of the saddle pommel. Now, at last, she had the dress shredded so she could tear off little pieces one at a time. She dropped a piece on the ground, then started preparing the next piece.

"Come on," Malloy growled, looking back at her. "If you can't keep up, I'll tie you belly-down across the saddle."

For a moment, Carmelita was frightened that perhaps Malloy had seen her drop the piece of cloth, but evidently he had not.

"I will keep up, señor," Carmelita promised.

She increased her pace slightly, but dropped another little piece of yellow cloth.

*Please, dear God,* she prayed silently. *Let my brother see the trail I am leaving for him. Let him find me and rescue me from this man.*

After Jim left Gonzales's Rancho del Rey, he found where the raiders had rejoined after the attack. There were a total of eight tracks, but he didn't know if that meant eight, or seven, men. If Carmelita was riding her own horse, it would mean seven men. If she was being carried by one of the men, it would mean eight.

He berated himself for the stupid mistake he had made. They had been so smart to set up a trap, to lure the attackers into the killing zone. But as it turned out, they were the ones who were suckered. While they were fighting in front of the house, Malloy had managed to sneak in from the rear and steal Carmelita.

About two miles north of the house, Jim saw that one set of tracks had veered off. Evidently, someone had circled around, intending to come up on his back trail.

Jim patted the neck of his horse, then stood in his stirrups and looked back along the trail he had just ridden. He couldn't see anyone, but he knew someone was back there.

"Well, horse, what do you think? Should I stop here and

wait on the fella tailing me? Or should I continue to follow the other tracks?''

Even as Jim was asking the question aloud, a small piece of yellow cloth caught his eye. He got off his horse, walked over, and picked it up. As soon as he examined it, he realized that it was from Carmelita's dress.

"Good for you, girl," he said, quietly. "You're leaving a trail."

Jim remounted and followed the tracks a while longer, where he found another piece of yellow cloth. The little bits of fabric were small and difficult to see, but there was no mistaking what they were. They were not only leading him to her, they were also indications that, for the moment, at least, she was still unhurt.

Jim had been riding for at least half an hour when he got the feeling that he was being watched. He twisted in his saddle to look behind him. Heat waves shimmered under the hot sun, but he saw no one.

The shot rang out shortly after he turned back around. The crack of the rifle and the deadly whine of lead searing the air reached his ears simultaneously. Only luck saved him: he had hunched in the saddle for a moment to adjust to the cantle just as the shot was fired. The bullet whizzed by where his head had been just an instant before.

Jim saw a puff of white smoke hanging in the air two hundred yards away. Flattening himself against his horse, he kicked it into a gallop and rode in a zigzag pattern toward the knoll below the little cloud of smoke. He drew his pistol and pointed it toward the spot just under the smoke. If so much as a hair showed above the crest, he would blast it. He covered the two hundred yards in about fifteen seconds, charged around the knoll, then jumped from his saddle and rolled on the ground toward the cover of a nearby rock.

There was no one there.

Jim lay behind the rock for a long moment until he was absolutely certain that he was alone. Then he moved cautiously over to where his ambusher had waited for him. On the ground was the spent cartridge of a .44-.40 jacked out of a Winchester by the assailant after firing. There were horse tracks nearby. His would-be assassin had fled.

# 10

The Cassias Lear Players closed their engagement in Buffalo Gap to the enthusiastic applause of an appreciative audience. In the dressing room backstage after the final performance, the actors, covered with a patina of perspiration and still in makeup, were experiencing the exhilaration of the moment.

Although it had been a long time since Artemus had been part of a professional theater group, he well understood the period of euphoria that could stay with one long after he or she left the stage. His belonging to this group of players was directly related to the investigation he and his partner were undertaking; yet even he was not immune to the ebullience of the moment. He saw, also, that Molly was caught up in the excitement.

Cassias Lear was particularly generous with his praise.

"What a wonderful addition to our traveling troupe Mr. Wilkes and his niece have made," Lear said. "We have been playing before packed houses ever since they joined us, and word has already gone ahead to Belle Plain. It is my prediction that the audiences there will be even larger and more demonstrative."

"I think we should celebrate the close of our successful run here," Noble suggested.

"My sentiments exactly," Corey added.

Lear smiled. "Gentlemen and lady," he said, "I have already made arrangements for that. I have rented a private dining room at the hotel. Even now they are filling the table with delightful things to eat and drink." He held his hand out in invitation. "Shall we go?"

"Drink? Bacchus shall has nothing on this poor player tonight," Noble said as he started toward the door.

The others started as well, but Lear hung back.

"Mr. Lear, you are not joining us?" Artemus asked.

"I must make arrangements for our train to proceed to the next place."

Artemus knew that Lear was using the word "train," in this instance, not in reference to the railroad, but in reference to the multitude of material that accompanied the troupe from town to town and theater to theater. This included everything from scores of costumes to musical instruments, stage weapons, props of sorts, and even flats. The latter was to enable them to construct a stage no matter where they might be, whether a saloon, a church, a grand concert hall, or a tent.

"I'll take care of it for you, Mr. Lear," Fitzhugh offered.

"No, I'll do it myself. You join the others," Lear said.

Artemus thought it rather odd that Lear did not let Fitzhugh, who was the stage manager, handle the shipping arrangements. He made a mental note to remember that.

Artemus and Molly joined the others in the walk from the theater to the private dining room Lear had arranged for them.

"Now, here is the task," Noble said as he poured wine into six goblets. "You are to drink every glass of wine, then return the glass to the table without spilling a drop."

"That doesn't sound all that difficult," Molly said.

"Ah, my dear, but you must do it with your hands behind your back," Noble added.

Molly laughed. "Then that will be difficult."

"I'll accept your beastly challenge," Corey said. He put his hands behind his back, then bent at the waist and, picking up the glass with his mouth, drained the first goblet, then returned it to the table.

"Bravo! But, can you do that five more times?" Noble asked.

Corey accepted the challenge, and performed the task perfectly.

Before they were more than half an hour into the party, Lear arrived, having made all the arrangements.

"We saved some food for you, Mr. Lear," Fitzhugh said as Lear sat at the table to join them.

"And the way you eat, Mr. Fitzhugh, that was no easy task," Corey teased, and the others laughed.

Lear and Fitzhugh sat at the table with the others and nodded their approval as a plate and glass were put before him.

"Did you get all the shipping arrangements made?" Artemus asked.

"Yes, thank you," Lear said. Lear took a swallow of his wine and studied Artemus thoughtfully over the rim of the cup. "Tell me, Mr. Wilkes, what is your interest in our train?"

"Just curious, Mr. Lear, just curious. I may want to start my own theater group some day. If so, I shall need to know every aspect of successful operation."

"Indeed," Lear said. Noticing that Artemus's glass was empty, Lear poured him another glass. "Tell me about your theater experience, Mr. Wilkes. I am quite impressed with your talent and wonder where else you have played."

"My most recent experience was with Edwin Booth," Artemus said.

At Edwin Booth's name, Lear's hand jerked and he poured wine over Artemus's hand and down onto the table-cloth. A dark, red stain spread across the linen.

"I'm sorry, Mr. Lear," Artemus said. "I must've jerked my hand." He knew that it had not been *his* hand that jerked, but, for the moment, he didn't want to put Lear off.

"That's . . . that's quite all right," Lear said. He handed Artemus a towel. "You appeared with Edwin Booth, you say?"

"Yes. Edwin is quite a talent. It is a shame that his brother brought such disgrace upon the family. The more so because of the Booth family of actors, John Wilkes was the least talented."

"Oh?" Lear said. "Well now, that surprises me. I always thought John Wilkes Booth was the most talented."

"You knew him? You saw him act?"

"Uh . . . no, I never met the man, nor did I ever see him perform," Lear said. "I was merely going by some of the things I have heard."

"His delivery was overly dramatic, his acting, if you can call it that, was wooden, and he was clumsy on the stage." Artemus forced a laugh. "Why, he couldn't even do a simple thing like leap down from the presidential box after he shot Lincoln. He caught his spur on the flag, then fell so awkwardly that he broke a bone in his leg. They would have never caught him, if he hadn't been slowed down with his broken leg."

"Then you are convinced that he was caught?" Lear asked.

"Of course he was caught and killed," Artemus said. "Why would you ask such a question? Do you think he wasn't caught?"

"I don't know," Lear replied. "One does hear rumors, from time to time."

"What sort of rumors?"

"Rumors that he may yet be alive."

Artemus laughed out loud. "One can hear stories of fairies dancing in the garden, too, but they are only stories. No, sir, John Wilkes Booth is dead. Of that, I am positive. And believe me, not only the country, but the theater is the better for it."

Lear took another swallow of his wine and studied Artemus for a long moment as he did so.

"Mr. Wilkes, may I inquire as to your politics?"

"My politics? Oh, I suppose I am Democrat when the candidate suits me to be so, and Republican if that candidate catches my fancy. Why do you ask?"

"I don't mean that kind of politics," Lear said. "I be-

101

lieve you mentioned that you are from Georgia, and your family lost everything during the War Between the States?''

''That's true. The house and land that had been in my family for five generations is now the home of some Yankee carpetbagger.''

''Then, you are not particularly sympathetic to the Union.''

''Sympathetic to the Union?'' Artemus said with a surprised look on his face. ''Hold on, sir, what are we talking about here? The war to settle that issue has been over for sixteen years. There is no going back; therefore, there is no need to even think about it.''

''Ah, but there is a means of going back,'' Lear suggested.

''And just how would you propose to do that?''

''Don't get me wrong, Mr. Wilkes. I am making no such proposal,'' Lear said. ''It isn't my place to do so. But, I am now the resident of a state which, by the unique circumstances of its entry into the Union, could, if it wished, secede from the United States, without the necessity of a war.''

''And the United States would just let it go?''

''Oh, I'm certain the United States would argue that, by its participation in the war, and by voluntarily becoming a state, Texas abrogated all the unique rights and privileges it realized as a sovereign nation. The issue would, no doubt, be taken to the Supreme Court.''

''And how do you think the Supreme Court would rule?''

''I believe they would not want to see the country thrown into another civil war so soon after the last. Therefore, I think the court would rule in our favor,'' Lear replied, quickly.

''*Our* favor?''

''Uh, that is, in favor of Texas, if Texas wanted to secede.''

''Tell me, Mr. Lear. Do you want to secede?''

Lear laughed. ''I am not a revolutionary, my dear fellow," he said. He poured himself another glass of wine. "I'm just making conversation."

"As was I, Mr. Lear," Artemus replied.

"Gentleman and lady," Lear began, holding his glass toward Molly, "I suggest we bring this celebration to a close, soon. We leave on the five o'clock train tomorrow morning. And I will expect you all there, on time, bright-eyed and ready to meet the public."

"To our continued success," Molly said, holding her glass aloft. The others looked at her with a stricken expression on their faces. "Did I say something wrong?" Molly asked, noticing the expressions.

"No, of course not, my dear," Artemus said, stepping into the silence. "It is just that it is bad luck to wish good luck."

"No problem," Fitzhugh said, easily. "She didn't wish us good luck, she merely offered a toast to our continued success. I see nothing wrong with that."

"Nor do I," Lear said. He held his glass out toward the others. "To our continued success."


Later that night, after the others had gone to bed, Artemus decided to have a closer look at the equipment that Lear had readied for shipping. The equipment was stacked in the railroad express room, which was at the opposite end of the depot.

The depot was dark, except for one small light in the dispatcher's office. As Artemus walked by that office, he could hear the snoring of the night dispatcher.

When Artemus got to the express room, the door was locked. Reaching behind the lapel of his jacket, he pulled out a long pin. He used the pin to pick the lock, and had the door open almost as quickly as if he had been using a key.

"How did you do that?" Molly asked. Surprised by her sudden appearance, Artemus jumped.

"Don't sneak up on a person like that," he hissed.

"Would you rather I have called out to you?" Molly teased.

"What are you doing here, anyway?"

"Same thing you are," Molly said. "This afternoon I saw something that made me curious. I wanted a closer look."

"What did you see?"

"A platen," Molly said.

"A what?"

"A platen," Molly said. "It's part of a printing press."

"Well, it wouldn't be all that unusual for them to have a printing press, I don't suppose," Artemus said. "They do put out a large number of handbills advertising our arrival. It would make sense to have their own press. In the long run, it would be a lot cheaper than hiring one."

"Yes, but this particular platen was exactly like the one that was on my father's printing press. If it is the same one, that would be evidence that they were involved with my father's death, wouldn't it?"

"Indeed it would," Artemus agreed.

Artemus lit a candle he was carrying and, in the flickering light, examined the equipment that was assembled for shipment. They began moving crates and flats around until Molly thought she saw something.

"There," she said. "There it is!" Molly pointed, and Artemus moved some boxes aside to get a better look.

The press was disassembled, but even in its disassembled state, it took up a lot of room. It was a heavily built contraption of cast iron with a wide bed and a sturdy frame. Molly examined the platen closely. "It's not it," she said. She stood up with disappointment on her face. "It's not the platen that was on my father's printing press."

Artemus examined the press. "Do you know much about printing presses?" he asked.

"I know a little," Molly answered. "I used to help my father around the shop."

"What about this press? Is this the kind of press one would have to print handbills?" Artemus asked.

"Handbills? Well, I should say so," Molly replied. "Why, you can put out newspapers from a press like this. In fact, my father did. And not only newspapers, but any kind of printing you could imagine: woodcuts, delicate certificates. This is an R. Hoe and Company Washington handpress. There is practically no job beyond its capability.''

Molly reached up to touch the tympan. ''Whoever used the press last didn't do a very good job of cleaning it, though. There is some ink left.''

Artemus put his finger on the ink to see if it was dry. It was still a little tacky, and some got onto his finger.

''I guess it's the old newspaperman's daughter in me,'' Molly said. ''But I hate to see a press this fine that isn't properly cleaned.''

Artemus heard something, and quickly extinguished the candle.

''What is it?'' Molly asked.

''Shh!'' Artemus said. ''Somebody is coming.''

Artemus put his hand on Molly's shoulder, and guided her over to one corner of the room. When the door opened, a soft wedge of light spilled in from the gas lantern outside. Someone stepped inside, and though it was too dark to make out any features, Artemus could see that whoever it was, was holding a gun.

''Who is in here?''

''Close your eyes,'' Artemus whispered. ''Close them very tightly and keep them shut.''

''All right, they're shut,'' Molly whispered back.

''I know someone is in here, and if you don't speak up, I'm going to start shooting!'' the man in the door said. He pulled back the hammer on his pistol, and the sound of the engaging sear sounded quite loud in the dark room.

Artemus pulled a small, billiard ball-sized sphere from his pocket. He threw it on the floor just in front of whoever had just come in. The ball shattered, activated a fuse, and released a quantity of phosphorous powder. The result was a blinding flash of light.

The man in the doorway shouted in surprise and alarm. Dropping his pistol, he covered his eyes with his arms.

''Come on, Fred,'' Artemus said, disguising his voice. ''He'll be blind for at least three minutes.''

''Who are you? What are you doing in here?'' the

blinded man shouted. He tried to take a step forward but the light had so blinded him that he couldn't move without bumping into something.

Because Artemus and Molly had both closed their eyes at the appropriate time, neither of them were suffering from flash blindness. As a result, they were able to pick their way by the intruder quite easily. They slipped by him, then, reaching the open air, ran, quickly, back to the hotel.

Artemus escorted Molly up to her room. She leaned against the wall beside the door, laughing, as she tried to regain her breath.

"That was fun!" she said. "And how clever of you to blind him in such a way."

"From time to time, I have learned that a trick up one's sleeve can be quite effective. He was an innocent night watchman doing his job," Artemus said. "I didn't want to hurt him."

Molly laughed. "I think you hurt only his pride."

"The printing press we found—could a person use it to print counterfeit money?" Artemus asked.

"Sure, if it was properly adapted," Molly said.

"Adapted? What do you mean, adapted?"

"In order to do fine printing—printing of engraved work, such as counterfeit money—you would have to have templates and frames to hold the engravings. I didn't see anything like that with the press. And, of course, the most important thing would be the plates themselves."

"They are there, somewhere," Artemus said.

"What makes you think so?"

"Did you see the last set of posters we sent out?"

"Yes, I saw them."

"What color were they."

"What color? Black print on white paper. Why do you ask?"

Artemus held out his finger, the finger that he had touched to the ink.

"Does this look like the ink they would have used?"

There, under the gaslight in the hall just outside Molly's door, she could see the ink quite plainly.

"Where did you get that ink?" she asked.

"From the tympan," Artemus replied.

"It's green," Molly said.

"Yes, it is green," Artemus agreed. "It is, in fact, the same shade of green as paper money."

# 11

"Let's hold up here for a minute, men," Malloy said. He stood in his stirrups and looked around. "Foster! Foster, are you here?" he called.

A rider appeared from behind a small ridge. "I'm here," he said. He saw Carmelita. "Who's the girl?"

"She's the sister of Ricardo Gonzales," Malloy answered.

Foster sighed. "If we want the people of Texas to support Texas liberation, we can't go around capturing innocent young women."

"She's a Mex."

"She's a young woman who is of no danger to the movement," Foster said. "At least, not until now. I'm telling you, this wasn't a smart thing to do."

"You are in charge of politics, Mr. Foster, I'm in charge of the military. You do your job and I'll do mine."

"That's just it," Foster replied. "The way you do your job makes it harder for me to do mine."

"What do you propose that I do? Turn her loose?"

"That might be a start."

"Not on your life," Malloy said. "Did you bring any grub?" he asked, changing the subject.

"I've got a pot of beans cooking," Foster said.

"Good. All right, men, we'll camp here for the night. Deke, take the first watch."

From the position of the stars, Jim supposed that it was about two in the morning. He had been sleeping, but something woke him up. He lay quietly for a few minutes, listening to the sounds in the night. Wind sighed through the dry limbs of a nearby mesquite tree, his horse blew and stamped its foot, but everything else was silent. Still, something had awakened him.

Quietly, Jim moved away from his sleeping roll. He crawled over to a small depression, slipped down into it, and looked back at his blankets. From this position, it looked as if someone was still sleeping there.

Suddenly there was a series of pistol shots. By the light of the muzzle flashes, Jim saw the face of the man who had been trailing him. It was gaunt, with high cheekbones, almost as if it were a skull, tightly covered by skin. He also saw a long, jagged scar running like a purple lightning flash from just below his left eye down to the corner of his mouth. From point-blank range, the bullets raised puffs of dust as they plowed into the sleeping roll. Jim realized that if he had still been sleeping, he would be dead now.

"Guess you won't be trailin' anyone now," the shooter said, his voice sounding thin in the night air, following as it did the crashing crescendo of pistol shots.

Jim waited to see if his nocturnal assailant would go over to check the bedroll, but he did not. Instead, a moment later Jim heard the sound of hoofbeats drumming against the hard, rocky ground. Whoever it was, was making a hasty retreat without checking to see whether or not he had been successful.

Jim decided to let him get away. If the assailant thought Jim was dead, he might be less cautious, and the trail would be easier to follow.

Jim's hunch was right. The man he was trailing did get a little more careless. Jim was able to pick up the trail quite easily after daylight, and he smiled broadly when he saw, by the tracks he was following, that the man had rejoined the others. He also found where they had camped for the night. Another small piece of yellow assured him that Carmelita was still alive.

"Hey!" one of the men behind Carmelita suddenly shouted. "What are you doing?"

Malloy, who was riding in front, stopped and looked around. "What is it?"

"This here señorita is playing us for the fool, Colonel. Look at her dress! You know what she's been doin'?"

When Malloy looked at Carmelita's bright yellow dress, he could see that a big piece had been torn from it.

"Well, now, if I had to guess, I would say she has been leaving little pieces of her dress behind," Malloy said.

"She's been leavin' little pieces . . ." the rider started to say, then, when he realized that Malloy had beat him to what he was going to say, he stopped in mid-sentence. "Yeah, that," he said, his voice trailing away.

"Take off the dress, girly," Malloy said.

"What? Señor, I will not!" Carmelita said.

"Oh, yeah, you'll take it off," Malloy said, easily. "Because if you don't, I'll have Deke take it off of you. You don't want that, do you?"

"I . . . I can't take off my dress. I'll have nothing to wear."

"Mr. Pippen, have you got an extra pair of pants and shirt in your roll?"

"Yeah, why?" Pippen asked.

"You're not much bigger'n the girl. Give your extra pants and shirt to her."

"Why would I want to do that? I just got 'em cleaned," Pippen complained.

"Just do it, Pippen," Malloy said with a long-suffering sigh. "I don't know why I didn't think of this earlier, anyway. That yellow dress of yours stands out like someone flashing a mirror."

"I don't have any place to change clothes," Carmelita said when Pippen handed her the pants and shirt.

"Stand behind your horse," Malloy ordered. "I'll see to it that none of them look at you."

"Who will see to you?" Carmelita asked.

"You can't have everything, girly," Malloy said. "Now, get changed."

Putting her horse between herself and the others, Carmelita took off her dress, then her petticoat. She stuck bare legs down into the pants Pippen had given her, then put on the shirt, thankful that she didn't have to show any more of herself than she did.

"Pete, that fella who was dogging our trail, the one you killed last night?" Malloy said.

"Yeah, what about him?"

"Was he Mex?"

Pete stroked the purple scar on his cheek. "I don't know."

Malloy looked at Pete in surprise. "What do you mean, you don't know? Was it too dark for you to see?"

"I didn't even look," Pete said. "I seen 'im asleep in his bedroll, so I let 'im have it, then I rode on."

"You idiot!" Malloy said.

"What is it? What's wrong?"

"How could you not check whether you even killed him or not?"

"Oh, I killed him, all right."

"How do you know you killed him?"

" 'Cause I pumped about six bullets into that bedroll, with him in it," Pete said. "Colonel . . . I wasn't no farther away from him than I am from you. I'm tellin' you, he's shot dead."

"But you don't know if he was Mex or not?"

"I don't know."

"Well, I don't plan to take any chances," Malloy said. "Especially since the girl has been leaving a trail. You, Clay, and Pippen, circle 'round to the west. Foster—you, Zeb and Jeter, go due north. Deke, you stay with me and the girl. We'll circle 'round to the east. That way, we'll have tracks goin' in three different directions. Anyone comin' after us won't know which set to follow."

"Since I'm goin' the most direct way, why don't you let the girl go with me?" Foster asked.

"The girl stays with me," Malloy said.

"What if she starts trying to leave another trail?" Deke asked.

"If she tries anything else, shoot her. Wait a minute," Malloy said. He smiled. "You have given me an idea."

"What kind of idea?"

Malloy laughed. "A *great* idea," he said.

When the trail split into three groups, Jim stopped and looked very carefully, trying to decide which trail he should follow. He started to go north, but a little piece of yellow cloth caught his eye in the trail that led off to the west.

"Good girl," he said, forking his horse off to the left.

Jim stayed on the trail for another five miles, then the tracks split again. This time one horse went one way, and the other two kept going. He didn't figure they had let Carmelita go, so he stayed on the trail of the two horses.

The pieces of yellow cloth were fewer and farther spaced now. He didn't know if she was being more cautious, or if she was just growing tired. Whatever the case, he figured he needed to catch up with her, so he urged his horse, which was by now growing trail weary, to a faster pace.

"I'm sorry, horse," Jim said. "But I've got to find them before they hurt the girl."

When Jim crested the next hill, he was rewarded by the sight of a flash of yellow in the trees ahead. It was the yellow dress!

Jim didn't know how much his horse had left, but there was no way he was going to let her out of his sight now. He slapped his legs against the animal's side and urged it into a gallop, rapidly closing the distance between them. When he was within one hundred yards of them, they stopped and turned toward him.

"What?" Jim shouted, jerking his horse to a halt. The person in the yellow dress wasn't Carmelita! It was a man, wearing Carmelita's dress. The cross-dresser and the other rider raised their rifles. Too late, Jim realized that he had been suckered, not only by this person wearing Carmelita's dress, but by the trail that had been left for him.

Both rifles cracked at the same time, and Jim heard the thunk of bullets hitting flesh as both bullets hit his horse. His horse whinnied once, then went down. When it did, it fell on Jim's leg. The soft part of the horse's belly gave way so that Jim's leg wasn't hurt, but he was momentarily pinned down by the weight of the animal.

When the two shooters saw that Jim was trapped, they turned and rode back toward him. He began wriggling around, trying to pull his leg free, but he couldn't do it.

"Well, now, you seem to have yourself in quite a fix there," one of the riders said. The one who spoke was the one in men's clothes.

"Yes, well, it was nice of you and your girlfriend to ride back to help me out," Jim said.

"Girlfriend?" the one in the dress growled.

"Take it easy, Pippen," the other man said, laughing. "He's just trying to make you mad."

"Yeah, well he's doin' a pretty good job of it. Tell him, Clay. Tell him, I ain't nobody's girlfriend."

"Who are you, mister?" Clay asked. "Why have you been chasin' us?"

"I'm with the Secret Service," Jim said.

"Secret Service?" Clay frowned. "What is that? I never heard of that."

"I'm a lawman," Jim said. "A federal lawman. You two are under arrest. So, if you would be so kind as to drop your guns and help me get out from under this horse . . ."

Clay and Pippen both laughed out loud.

"We're under arrest and you want us to drop our guns," Clay said. "There you are, lying on the ground under a dead horse, can't get loose, and can't get to your pistol, and you tell us we are under arrest. I'll give you this, mister. You got gall."

"Kill 'im, Clay," Pippen said. "Kill 'im, and get it over with."

Clay sighed. "Might as well," he said. He jacked another shell into his rifle, then raised it to his shoulder. "Say your prayers, mister federal lawman."

Jim flexed his arm, and as he did so, the small holdout gun he kept up his sleeve popped into his hand. Though the gun was small, it had two barrels, and it fired .41 caliber shells. He pulled the trigger just as Clay was tightening his finger on his own trigger. Jim's bullet caught Clay between the eyes, and he died before he even realized he was in danger.

"What the hell?" Pippen shouted. Realizing his own peril, he cocked his rifle and tried to raise it, but Jim discharged the second barrel before Pippen could do so. This bullet caught Pippen in the chest, and the yellow dress he was wearing turned red. Pippen fell from his horse.

As Jim worked to free himself from the horse, he could hear the labored breathing of Pippen as he lay dying. It was a little disconcerting, and Jim wished there could have been another way to handle the situation, but they had left him no choice.

By the time Jim had managed to free himself, Pippen, too, was dead.

The horses Clay and Pippen had been riding were well trained, and both were still standing there. Jim chose the better-looking of the two, then swung into the saddle.

"I hope you fellas don't mind me borrowing one of your horses," he said as he rode off.

Jim knew now what had happened. If Carmelita was still alive, and he was reasonably certain she was, then she had gone off with one of the other groups of riders. But it was a long way back to where the trail divided. It was somewhat shorter back to where the last rider had parted company with these two. And that man, whoever he was, was Jim's only connection to Carmelita. He slapped his legs against the side of his horse and urged him on.

"Let's go," he said to the horse. "I've got a few questions I want to ask this man."

Jim picked up the trail of the third rider, and followed it for another seven or eight miles. Then, in the distance before him, with heat waves shimmering under the punishing sun, he spotted a small village.

Jim dismounted, and led his horse over to a clump of trees. He removed the saddle.

"I might as well let you be comfortable for a while," he said to the grateful animal. "But it's nearly night, so I think I'll wait for dark before I take a look around down there."

The night creatures called to each other as Jim stood looking out toward the little village. A cloud passed over the moon and moved away, bathing in silver the little town that rose up like a ghost before him. A couple of dozen adobe buildings, half of which were lit up, fronted the town plaza. The biggest and most brightly lit building was the lone saloon at the far end of town.

Inside the saloon someone was playing a guitar, and Jim could hear the music beyond the edge of town. The player was good, and the music was a mournful, lonesome music, the kind of melody a man could let run through his mind during long, quiet rides.

Jim saddled the horse, but decided to put on a hobble and walk into town. He didn't particularly want to be seen, and he decided his arrival would be less noticeable if he arrived on foot. He checked his pistol. It was loaded and slipped easily from its sheath.

Jim started into town, caught the smell of beans and spicy beef from one of the houses, and realized that it had been a couple of days since he had eaten well. His stomach growled in protest.

A dog barked, a ribbony yap that was silenced by someone.

A baby cried, a sudden gargle that cracked the air like a bullwhip.

A housewife raised her voice in one of the houses, launching into a tirade about something, sharing her anger with all who were within earshot.

Though Jim normally walked down the middle of a street to avoid ambush from the shadows, this was an entirely different situation. This time the shadows, instead of being his enemy, were his ally. He moved through them, staying out of sight until he reached the saloon.

Jim listened to the sounds from the saloon. The music had stopped, and now there was only conversation. He froze when he recognized the voice of the man who had pumped five bullets into his sleeping roll the night before.

Jim stepped up onto the board porch and pushed his way inside. He pulled his hat brim low and headed for the bar, positioning himself in a way that put his back to the wall. He glanced around the room, then spotted the same purple-scarred face he had seen in the light of the muzzle flashes. The scar-faced man was standing at the far end of the bar.

"What'll it be?" the bartender asked.

"Give me a beer," Jim ordered.

The bartender put a glass under the barrel, pulled the spigot, then slid the foam-topped glass across the bar to Jim.

Jim picked up the glass and blew off some of the foam, all the while studying the scar-faced man in the mirror. Finally, his unwavering gaze caught the man's attention.

"Mister, you been lookin' at me ever since you come in here," the scar-faced man said in an irritable voice.

"Have I?" Jim asked.

"Yeah, you have. And I don't much like it."

"It's funny the way some people are," Jim said. "Now, you take you, for example. You don't like being stared at. On the other hand, I don't like having someone sneak up on me in the middle of the night to shoot five holes into their sleeping roll."

It wasn't until that moment that the man realized who Jim was. "What the . . . ? Mister, what does it take to kill you?" he shouted, his hand dipping for his gun.

Jim slipped his own pistol out quick as a snake and for one frozen instant in time, he and scar-face stood looking at each other, pistols drawn.

All other sound and activity ceased. Then the room was shattered with the roar of two pistols exploding. The other patrons yelled and dived or scrambled for cover. White gunsmoke billowed out in a cloud that filled the center of the room, momentarily obscuring everything.

As the smoke began to clear, the scar-faced man stared through the white cloud, smiling broadly at Jim. He opened his mouth as if to speak, but the only sound he made was a gagging rattle way back in his throat. The smile left his face, his eyes glazed over, and he pitched forward, his gun clattering to the floor.

Jim stood ready to fire a second shot if needed, but a second shot wasn't necessary. He looked down at the man for a moment, then holstered his pistol.

"Anybody know his name?" Jim asked. He looked around the saloon, studying every face. All heads were shaking, and he didn't see an expression of recognition in any of them.

Jim searched through the outlaw's pockets and found forty dollars in gold and a hundred dollars in green. He looked at the bills, all twenties, and saw that they were all counterfeit.

Finding the counterfeit didn't help with the problem of rescuing Carmelita, but it did help with his investigation. If this person really was involved with the Texas Liberation Front, this would be the first time he had been able to make a physical connection between the Texas Liberation Front and counterfeiting. He put the greenbacks and the gold pieces in his pocket, then returned to the bar and tossed down the rest of the beer. At the other end of the bar he noticed a young boy, about twelve, who had been sweeping the floor. The boy was standing there, eyes open wide at the drama he had just witnessed.

"Boy," he called, pulling out half a dollar. "You know the stand of alamo trees just south of town?"

"Yes, sir," the boy said.

Jim tossed the fifty-cent piece to him. "You'll find my horse there. Bring him into town."

"Yes, sir!" the boy said, grinning broadly at the easy half-dollar. He scooted out the front door.

"Is there a hotel in this town?" Jim asked.

"Next door," the bartender answered.

"When the boy gets back with my horse, tell him where I am. Tell him to stable the horse."

Jim took out the two twenty-dollar gold pieces and put them on the bar, then he looked at the body of the man he had just killed.

"A couple of his partners are lying in the desert about ten miles south of here," he said. "Have the undertaker take a wagon out for them. He may as well bury all three of them together."

"Three pine boxes won't cost more'n nine dollars," the bartender said, sliding one of the coins back toward him. "Diggin' the graves, another six. Twenty dollars is enough."

"There an orphanage in town?"

"No orphanage, but Miz Phillips, she takes care of four or five kids that don't have any parents. The boy you just sent after your horse is one of 'em."

"Give the other twenty to her."

"How do you know to trust me?"

"You were going to give it back to me, weren't you? I figure you'll do the right thing."

"Yes, sir, I'll do it. You can count on it," the bartender said, taking the extra coin back.

# 12

Jim left town before dawn. It was mid-morning now, and the sun was a quarter of the way through its daily transit. Already the heat was fierce, and what little wind there was, was blowing against his face like a breath from the mouth of a blast furnace.

Ahead of him the brown land lay in empty folds of rocks, dirt, and dry scrub brush. The sun heated the ground, then sent up undulating waves that caused near objects to shimmer and nonexistent lakes to appear tantalizingly in the distance.

Jim picked up the tracks of three riders. The ground was hard, and the tracks so indistinct that he could tell very little about them. He didn't know if Carmelita was one of the riders or not.

Often, Jim would have to get down and examine the tracks very closely to make certain he was still on the right trail. That necessity saved his life, for just as he was dismounting, a rifle cracked and the bullet sizzled by, taking his hat off, fluffing his hair, and sending shivers down his spine.

In one motion, Jim was on the ground and had the pistol out of his holster. Not wanting to lose another horse to someone trying to kill him, he slapped his horse's flank to get him out of the line of fire, then dived for a nearby rock, just as a second shot came so close to his ear that he could hear the air pop as the bullet sped by.

Jim wriggled his body under cover, then raised himself slowly and looked over the top of the rock. He couldn't see anyone, but he did see a little puff of white smoke drifting slowly to the east. That meant the shooter had to be somewhat west of the smoke. When Jim shifted his eyes in that direction, he saw a hat rise slowly above the rocks.

Jim waited until he thought enough of the hat was visible to provide a target, then he shot. The hat went sailing away.

"Mister, you just put a hole in a twenty-dollar hat," a voice called out in anger.

"I'm really sorry about that," Jim replied. "I meant to put the hole in your head."

The marksman fired again and surprised Jim, because he had his eyes fixed right where he thought the man would have to come up. Somehow the man had managed to slip down the rock for a small distance.

This bullet was as close as the first one. It hit the rock right in front of Jim. It kicked tiny pieces of rock and shreds of hot lead into his face before it whined away behind him. Jim turned around and slid down to the ground, brushing the hot lead from his cheeks.

"You are the one that's been followin' us, ain't you?" the voice called. "I wouldn't want to go killin' the wrong fella."

"Are you Malloy?" Jim asked.

"Naw," the man answered. "Colonel Malloy, he's got the girl. He left me behind to take care of you."

"And who might you be?" Jim asked.

"The name is Deke Maxwell. I reckon you've heard that name before."

"No, can't say as I have."

In fact, Jim knew exactly who Deke Maxwell was. He was a young gunman trying to make a name for himself. He had killed a couple of well-known gunfighters who had all but retired because of age. Among those who didn't know better, the names of Deke Maxwell's victims managed to give Deke the reputation he so eagerly sought. But those who really knew, knew that the reputation was cheaply bought.

"Are you kidding me, mister? You really never heard of me?" Deke asked, obviously disappointed by Jim's reply.

"Am I supposed to have heard of you?"

"You heard of Clint Morgan, ain't you? And Murphy Green?"

"I heard some punk kid dry-gulched them," Jim answered coldly. "Never heard the name of the punk who actually did it."

"What's your name, mister?" Deke asked.

"My name is Jim West. I'm an agent for the Secret Service."

Deke chuckled. "You mean you're a federal lawman?"

"That's right."

"Well, now, this is goin' to be real interestin'. I never killed me no federal lawman before."

"Would you care to step out from behind that rock and face me down?" Jim challenged.

"Sure, why not?" Deke called back. "I'll try you."

Jim looked around the rock and saw that Deke Maxwell was coming out from behind his cover with his pistol holstered and his hands spread out beside him. Jim holstered his own pistol, then stood up.

"I must confess, you surprised me," Jim said. "I didn't think you would do it."

"Maybe I got another surprise for you," Deke said, grinning evilly.

"You never can tell," Jim replied. "You might—" Jim's reply was interrupted by a pistol shot from his left. The bullet missed, though he didn't know how it could have, because he was so close to his assailant that he felt the sting of burnt gunpowder.

"Billy, you idiot, you missed!" Deke shouted as he went for his own gun.

Jim had a fifth of a second to make a decision. Should he fire his first shot at Deke, who was just now going for his gun, or at Billy, who was now rising up from behind a nearby rock with his gun already in his hand?

Jim decided to go for Deke. Despite the fact that he was ribbing the young gunsel, he knew shooting, and he knew that Deke was good. Billy had already demonstrated his inaccuracy in the missed opportunity an instant earlier.

Quick as thought, Jim's gun was cocked and booming. The bullet slammed into Deke's chest. Deke completed his draw and pulled the trigger, but he was already dead by the time his gun cleared his holster.

Even before Deke hit the ground, Jim was turning to fire at the other man, who was also firing. Billy's second shot proved as ineffective as his first, but Jim's bullet hit Billy in the hip, causing him to double over, then crumple down in pain.

Jim stood quietly for a moment as the echoes of the shots came rolling back from a nearby rock wall. When the last echo was a subdued rumble off a distant hill, the silence returned. The limbs of a nearby tree rustled in the breeze. A shock of tumbleweed bounced by, and a lizard scurried across a rock.

"Oh," Billy moaned. "Oh, this hurts. I've never had anything hurt like this."

"Where's Malloy?" Jim asked. "And the girl? Where's the girl?"

"I'm gut-shot, and you're standing there asking me questions," Billy said.

Jim looked at the wound. It was in the hip—painful, but probably not fatal.

"You aren't gut-shot."

"I'm going to die."

"You won't die," Jim said. "Unless I kill you. Now, where's Malloy?"

"I can't tell you that," Billy moaned.

"Have it your own way," Jim replied calmly. He held this pistol down toward Billy's head and cocked it.

"Are you . . . are you going to kill me?" Billy asked.

"Looks like it," Jim answered easily.

"No, wait!" Billy shouted. "Don't kill me."

"Where's the girl?" Jim asked again.

"You don't understand. Malloy will kill me if I tell you."

"Well now, if I were you, I'd think about that, Billy, because I'm here, and Malloy isn't. Now, where's the girl?"

"Look, this ambush business, this wasn't my idea," Billy explained. "It was Deke's notion. He's the one wanted to kill you." He looked down at his wound. "Damn," he said. "Maybe you're right. Maybe I ain't goin' to die after all. It's stopped bleedin', and it's quit hurting already."

Jim knew that the numbness would wear off and the pain would return, worse than before, but he said nothing about that.

"So . . . what are you going to do with me?" Billy asked.

"I'm going to use you to take a message to Malloy," Jim said.

"What message?"

"Tell him if he doesn't let the girl go, he is going to answer to me, personally."

"All right, I'll give him the message," Billy said. He stood up and limped over to the rock behind Deke's body. There were two horses tied there. He climbed up on one, then looked down at Jim.

"But you give me an hour's start. If you don't, the girl's dead . . . wolf meat. You savvy?"

"Oh yes, I quite understand," Jim said.

"You're lucky you didn't kill me. Colonel Malloy looks out for his men. If neither one of us had come back, he would'a killed the girl."

Jim watched Billy ride away, then he walked over to look down at Deke's body. Deke was slack-jawed and hollow-eyed in death. The expression of surprise was frozen on his face, and a little dribble of blood oozed from his mouth.

Jim decided to bury Deke while he waited for Billy to clear out. He dragged the body over to a small ravine and pushed it in, rolling it down the incline. He started to throw the rocks down on the body, then he happened to think that he should probably go through the man's pockets. He slid down into the ravine, knelt down, and ran his hand through the pockets. He pulled out a wad of greenbacks, nearly two hundred dollars. And every bill was counterfeit.

# 13

As the train raced through the night, conversation stilled as many of the passengers began trying to find some way to get comfortable in their seats. The conductor had helped the situation by dimming all the lanterns so that, although the car wasn't in total darkness, it was in shadow.

Artemus, who was sitting with Molly, was watching Cassias Lear from the corner of his eye.

"I've got to get into the baggage car and have a look around," Artemus whispered to Molly. "If those plates are on board this train, I intend to find them."

"How are you going to do that?" Molly asked. "If you leave and are gone too long, Lear will get suspicious."

"Then I'll just have to do something that will alleviate his suspicion," Artemus said. He looked at the narrow mirror that separated the two windows beside the facing seats. "Hmm, that's interesting," he said.

"What?"

"Do you have a small mirror with you?"

Molly smiled. "Of course I have a small mirror. What woman would ever be without one?"

"Let me borrow it for a moment."

Molly took a mirror from her handbag and gave it to Artemus. He held the mirror out, turning it at several different angles, studying it and its reflection in the larger mirror that separated the windows.

"What on earth are you doing?" Molly asked.

"I am establishing the correct optic angles," Artemus replied.

"Optic angles?"

"Yes."

Without further explanation, Artemus put the mirror in the seat across from him, then adjusted the angle very carefully. Sitting back in his own seat, he studied the arrangement for a minute.

"Yes, that will work."

"What will work?" Molly asked, almost frustrated now by her deepening curiosity and Artemus's maddening silence to her questions.

"When I get up, I want you to move away from the window," Artemus said. "Sit here, in the aisle seat, where I am sitting."

"You want to change seats? I'd be glad to."

"Yes, and no," Artemus said. "That is, I'm going to be sitting in the window seat, but not really."

Molly sighed. "And I'll tell you something else you are really not doing. You are really not making any sense."

"Have you ever viewed pictures through a stereoscope?"

"Yes. Oh, they are wonderful. The pictures are so lifelike."

"Have you ever seen a magic lantern show?"

"You mean, where pictures are projected onto a screen? Yes, I have seen those as well."

"Good, then you understand the principle. What I plan to do is use a magic lantern to project an image of me sitting in that seat. And, by using these two mirrors to split the image, it will create a figure with depth, just as a stereoscope does."

"Can you do that?"

"Yes. But in order to make it real, you are going to have to pretend to be carrying on a conversation with that image."

"Oh, I can do that."

Artemus shook his head. "It won't be as easy as you think. For you, there won't even be a picture. All you will see is the light. In order to get the full effects of the image, you would have to be viewing it from behind, by several feet."

"You mean, where Mr. Lear is now?"

"Yes."

"How are you going to set it up without him seeing what you are doing?"

"I'm going to have to think about that for a moment," Artemus said. He stood up and stretched. "I'll be back in a few moments, my dear," he said in a voice that was loud enough for Lear to hear.

Artemus disappeared through the front of the train. A few moments later, a bearded and bespectacled man wearing the hat of a railroad official came walking down the aisle from the front of the car, carrying a case. He stopped about a fourth of the way down, then leaned over and adjusted one of the lanterns.

"Is this about right?" he asked the passenger there. "Is the lantern too bright, too dim, or just right?"

"What are you doing? I was asleep," the passenger complained.

"Very good, sir, I'll just leave it as it is," the official said.

The man shuffled on down the aisle, occasionally making an adjustment to the lanterns, and exchanging a few words with the passengers. He reached Molly.

"And what about you, my dear?" he asked. "It seems much too bright here. Wouldn't you like me to extinguish this lantern?"

The man winked at her. For a second, Molly was angry. How dare this man be so brazenly forward as to think she would welcome such an advance? Then, when he winked a second time, she realized that it was Artemus. How had he undergone such a dramatic change in his appearance so quickly?

"The lantern, madam. Shall I extinguish it for you?"

Molly realized then that he would need darkness for his magic lantern projection, so she assented. "Yes, it is a little bright here," she said.

"I just spoke to your uncle," Artemus said. "He is getting a breath of fresh air on the vestibule. He told me to tell you he will be back shortly."

"Thank you," Molly said.

Artemus extinguished the lantern, then went to the very back of the car. Cassias Lear was sitting in the last seat of the car, and Artemus put his case down on the seat beside Lear.

"I hope you don't mind, sir. I need to do a little work with this one," Artemus said.

"There's nothing wrong with that lantern," Lear said. "It is fine."

"Oh, my, you are one of those theater people, aren't you?" Artemus said. He took out a projector and mantle as he talked. "Yes, I saw you do . . . *Macbeth*, I believe it was. What a marvelous job you did. 'Tomorrow, and tomorrow, and tomorrow, creeps in this petty pace, day to day . . .' "

"Yes, yes, I know the soliloquy," Lear said impatiently.

"Oh, indeed, I should say you do," Artemus said. "How beautifully you performed that night." He put the slide holder in front of the lantern, then turned the lantern up.

"What are you doing? Since you put that shade on it, there's less light now than there was," Lear said.

"I know," Artemus said. "It's awful, isn't it? It's a new device the railroad is making us try. They seem to think that by putting a mantle over the lantern, we can diffuse the light, thus making one lantern do the work of two or three. They are trying to save money."

"Everyone is trying to save money these days," Lear grumbled. "Whatever happened to old-fashioned service?"

"Indeed, sir, that is exactly what I say," Artemus replied. He moved the projected beam slightly, then picked up the two mirrors. The effect was just as he had hoped: he had a picture of himself on a glass slide. By using the glass slide in conjunction with the magic lantern, he had projected a lifesize photograph of himself onto the two mirrors. The mirrors caught the beam, split it, then reconstructed the image so that the effect was startling. From here it looked as if Artemus was actually sitting in the seat between Molly and the window.

"Oh, I see that the young lady's uncle is back in his seat," Artemus said. "Perhaps I should see if he needs anything."

"That's odd," Lear said. "I didn't see him come back to his seat."

"Didn't you?" Artemus asked. "Well, you and I were engaged in conversation, so I suppose his return just slipped your notice."

"My dear sir, *we* weren't engaged in conversation," Lear said irritably. "I was listening to your prattling monologue."

"Yes, I suppose it might have appeared that way," Artemus said. "Well, I shan't bother you anymore. I've many more cars and lanterns to see to. Have a pleasant trip, sir."

Artemus closed his case, then started forward toward the baggage car.

"You just came from that direction," Lear pointed out.

Artemus paused only a second before he came up with what he hoped was a plausible explanation. "Yes, I did, sir. I started here first."

As Artemus passed the seat where Molly was sitting next to the projected image, he stopped and looked. If he had not seen the image from the back of the car, he would be worried. For from here, he could see nothing but a bright splash of light.

"Ah, I see your uncle is back. How about you, sir? Is the light about right for you?" Artemus put his hand to his ear. "Beg pardon, sir? I didn't hear you. Oh, very good, sir, I'm glad you are pleased. Do have a pleasant evening, sir. You too, miss."

As Artemus moved on toward the front of the car, he looked back one more time to see how Lear had taken his little performance. Evidently, Lear was satisfied, for he was now sitting quietly, staring through the window at the blackness outside. He smiled when he saw that Molly appeared to be engaged in conversation with the dull glow of light to her right.

It was dark in the baggage car, but Artemus was able to find and light a lantern. He adjusted it until a bubble of golden light filled the car. That was when he saw the stage manager, Fitzhugh, sitting on the floor with his back to the wall.

"Fitzhugh! What are you doing here?" Artemus asked, startled to see him and thinking quickly to come up with a reason for his own presence.

"Wilkes," Fitzhugh gasped. "I've been stabbed." Fitzhugh had been holding his hand across his chest, and when he pulled it away, Artemus could see that a pool of blood had collected in his palm. In addition, the whole front of his chest was covered with blood.

"Who did this?" Artemus asked, opening the shirt to see if he could stem the flow of blood.

"I don't know. It was dark. I couldn't see." Fitzhugh gasped a couple of times. "My real name is Charles Garrison. I'm a Texas Ranger. I want you to get word to Captain Bailey."

"Captain Bailey, yes. I'll get word to him about you."

"No, it's too late for me. This is about the president."

"The president? You mean *the* president? President Garfield?"

"Tell him . . ." Fitzhugh started, then he tried to cough. He coughed once, then he gasped one last breath and died.

Artemus stood up and looked down at the body. So the Texas Rangers were on this case. It was too bad that he and the man he had known as Fitzhugh had not known about each other. They could have covered each other's backs.

The fact that a Texas Ranger had infiltrated the group told Artemus that he and Jim were not the only ones to have been suspicious. The fact that the Texas Ranger had been killed meant that their suspicions were valid. However, it also told him that he would have to be very, very careful.

Artemus looked through the baggage car then, searching not only the props and flats that supported the production, but also searching through the suitcases and trunks. He searched for at least thirty minutes, but found nothing. Finally, frustrated at his inability to turn up anything he could use, he extinguished the lantern and left the baggage car. He felt a little uneasy about leaving Garrison's body behind, but he couldn't do anything about it without exposing himself. Besides, he reasoned, Garrison was dead. There was nothing more Artemus could do for him.

When Artemus returned to the car, he saw that Lear was asleep. Very quietly, he walked back to the lantern, extinguished it, then removed the glass slide that contained his image.

"What?" Lear asked. "What are you doing?"

"This lantern was too bright," Artemus said. "I turned it down. I hope you don't mind."

Lear grunted, then closed his eyes and went back to sleep.

The next morning, as the train stood in the depot at Trinity Mills, a wagon was backed up to the baggage car. Two men loaded the body of the man Artemus now knew was Garrison onto the wagon. A sign on the side of the wagon read Prufrock Undertaking Services.

One of the porters had discovered the body just after dawn, and as soon as the train had reached the small town of Trinity Mills, the sheriff was contacted. The sheriff had called the entire troupe together, and was now talking with them.

"You are Cassias Lear?" the sheriff asked.

"I am, sir," Lear replied. "I am the head of this little band of players."

"And who are you?"

"Noble. Jason Noble, at your service," Noble answered with a sweeping bow.

"And I, sir, am Malcolm Corey. This is a terrible tragedy

for us. I hope you can discover who did it.''

"Yes," Lear said. "Mr. Corey is right. It is indeed a tragedy, for Mr. Fitzhugh was our stage manager. Now I will have to assume his tasks. Do you have any idea how difficult it is to act and direct, as well as perform all the duties as stage manager? It is a herculean task.''

"I'm sure it is," the sheriff said. "And I can see how broken up you are by Mr. Fitzhugh's death.''

"My relationship with Mr. Fitzhugh was business only," Lear said. "We weren't exactly friends.''

"Well, if you weren't friends, were you enemies?''

"No, we were not. And I will not have you putting words into my mouth, Sheriff," Lear said.

"What about you? Who are you?" the sheriff asked Artemus.

"I am Horatio Wilkes. And this is my niece, Claire Wilkes.''

"Did you get along with Fitzhugh?" the sheriff asked.

"I hardly knew the man," Artemus answered. "My niece and I only recently joined the troupe.''

"They are telling the truth, sheriff," Lear said. "If you are looking for the murderer, I am afraid you are going to have to look somewhere else.''

"Do you have any suggestions as to where that might be?''

"Mr. Fitzhugh was a gambler, who also had a propensity to drink. That is a dangerous combination. And last night I saw him both drinking and playing cards," Lear said. "Is it not inconceivable that he got into a fight over a card game? This is the wild West after all, and such things do happen.''

"I don't suppose you could describe who he was playing cards with, could you?" the sheriff asked.

Lear shook his head. "Perhaps one of the others saw him as well. If so, ask them to describe the players. They were ruffian-type men, and all ruffians look alike to me.''

The sheriff sighed. "You aren't being much help.''

"I'm sorry," Lear said. "Dealing with murder is a little out of my line. I am an actor.''

"Yes, so you said. Tell me, Mr. Lear, how long are you going to be in Trinity Mills?"

"We will have a three-day run here," Lear said. "Why do you ask?"

"I just want to know how to get hold of you, in case I have any more questions," the sheriff said. "I don't want you disappearing on me."

"Look at us, Sheriff," Lear said. "Do we look as if we could disappear?"

As always, the actors were dramatically dressed, with flowing capes, the capes lined in brightly colored silk, high hats, and three-piece suits. Molly wasn't in a suit, but the dress she was wearing was nothing like the work dresses and aprons most of the women of Trinity Mills were wearing. As a result, she stood out among the women as dramatically as did the actors stand out among the men of the town.

The sheriff chuckled. "I suppose you have a point there," he said.

"Are you through with us, now?" Lear asked.

"Yeah, I'm through." He looked over toward the body, which was now loaded onto the wagon. "Hold on there, Prufrock. I want another look at the body." The sheriff hurried over to the wagon.

"What do we do now, Mr. Lear?" Noble asked.

"Mr. Noble, you see to getting us checked into the hotel," Lear said. "I will make the arrangements to have our luggage and equipment transported to the theater."

"I can get everything over there for you if you'd like," Artemus offered.

"No, thank you. I'll see to it myself," Lear replied.

"Very well, if you insist." Artemus started walking away.

"Where are you going?" Lear asked.

"I thought I'd take a walk around the town, get a good look at it," Artemus said.

"Go with Noble."

"I'm sure Mr. Noble doesn't need my help to get us all checked into the hotel."

"I think, under the circumstances, it would be better if we all stayed together," Lear suggested. "After all, we don't know who killed Mr. Fitzhugh. It could be some crazed person who has a personal vendetta of some sort against people of the theater."

"Don't worry, Mr. Lear. I'll keep us together," Noble promised.

*The White House, Washington, D.C.*

President James A. Garfield rested his elbows on his desk and pinched the bridge of his nose.

"How many more are out there, Walter?" he asked his appointments secretary.

"About forty, I believe, Mr. President," Walter answered.

Garfield sighed. "All seeking some sort of patronage appointment?"

"I'm afraid so, sir."

"That's what comes from being a compromise candidate," Garfield said. "The Republican Party split into two groups, the Stalwarts and the Half-breeds. And because I was a compromise, they all want their pound of flesh from me."

"I believe these are all Stalwarts, sir," Walter said. "They have been coming out in droves since Senators Conkling and Platt resigned their seats in protest, claiming that you were favoring the Half-breeds."

"I'm not favoring either group, Walter," Garfield said. "If I had my way, I would do away with patronage altogether." He stood up and walked over to the window to look out over the city.

"What shall I do with those who are waiting, sir?"

"Send them home," Garfield said with a dismissive wave of his hand. "Send them all home, and tell the staff to turn them away from now on. Beginning tomorrow, appointments will be made on merit, not for political payback."

"Mr. President, you are going to make a great deal of enemies, I fear."

Garfield turned away from the window and smiled. "Walter, I was a major general in the army during the Civil War. The enemies I had then were trying to kill me. Do you really think I'm going to worry about stepping on a few political toes now?"

Walter laughed. "I guess not, sir."

"Now, where was that invitation?"

"Invitation, sir?"

"Yes, you know the one. Governor Oran Roberts, of Texas, has invited me to meet him in Dallas. It seems the good citizens of Dallas are going to have a three-day celebration of our nation's birthday this year. There will be a reception, a special theatrical showing, and something called a rodeo. Do you know what a rodeo is?"

"I'm afraid not, sir."

"Evidently, it is a display of cowboy skills: riding, roping, shooting, bullfighting, and the like. I must say, I'm rather looking forward to it. It will be nice going out West for a small vacation. I can't be doing too badly, can I, when a Republican president receives such an invitation from a governor who is a Democrat?"

"I would say that is a sterling endorsement, sir," Walter said. "But what about your class reunion at Williams College?"

"Oh, I had forgotten about that."

"Shall I cancel it?"

"No, not yet."

"You won't be able to attend both of them, Mr. President."

"Don't give up on me, Walter," Garfield said. "As you know, I can write Greek with my left hand, and Latin with my right. Anyone who can do that can surely find a way to attend both events."

# 14

Carmelita lay on a cot and stared at the ceiling above her, trying to focus her thoughts. She concentrated on where she was, and on how long she had been with this man who seemed to control her every move. He told her when she should ride and when she should rest, when she could eat and when she could sleep. It seemed as if he had always been in control of her life . . . as if she had no memory of the time before she was with him; and yet, it had only been three days since she had been taken from her brother's house.

She thought of the last three days, recalling the hours of riding in the hot sun and through the dark of night, the anger of Malloy as he learned that, one by one, his men were being killed off.

Where was her brother? Was he coming for her? Was he the one killing Malloy's men? Or was it the Anglo, the one called West?

She had danced for James West, and had felt pleasure in doing so. Recalling that pleasure now was the only respite she had from this trying ordeal.

Foster came into the room then, carrying a tray with steaming beans and a cup of coffee. He put it on the table beside her bed.

"I thought you might be hungry," Foster said.

"*Gracias, señor,*" Carmelita said. She began eating, and because it was late in the day and this was the first time she had eaten that day, the beans seemed exceptionally good.

"Are you all right?" Foster asked.

"Do you really care whether I'm all right or not?" Carmelita replied.

"Yes, I do. I wouldn't have asked, otherwise."

"Then I will tell you, I am not all right. And I will not be all right until I am free."

Foster rubbed his chin. "Yeah, well, if it was up to me, I wouldn't have captured you," he said. "Malloy had no business doing that."

"Who are you?" Carmelita asked. "You are not like the others."

"My name is Foster. I'm the political officer of the Texas Liberation Front."

"The Texas Liberation Front," Carmelita said. She spat disgustedly. "It is no army. It is a bunch of cowards. They fight only unarmed people."

Foster chuckled. "From what I hear, your brother wasn't unarmed. Malloy came out the worse for that little spat. He lost five men out at the ranch, and whoever has been trailing him has accounted for five more. And all Malloy has to show for his little raid is you."

"Señor Foster, let me go. I beg of you."

"I can't," Foster said uneasily. "At least, not yet. But I will watch out for you the best I can. In the meantime, whatever Malloy tells you to do, you do, without fighting him. I don't have to tell you, he is a very evil person."

It was late afternoon when Jim approached the town of Puxico. He had ridden in from the southwest, following the railroad into town. The depot platform was empty, but Jim saw a pump at the far end of the platform, and he rode straight to it. Getting down from his horse, he gave the handle a couple of jerks and held his head under the spout. He let the water run over him. When his head was thoroughly drenched, he raised up and wiped his face with his kerchief and smoothed his hair with his fingers.

"I expect the water feels good after a long ride," someone said. The speaker was an older man with gray hair and a long, gray beard. He was wearing a railroad hat.

"Sure does," Jim agreed. "You the stationmaster?"

"I'm the freight clerk."

"Mr. Freight Clerk, I'm looking for a town called Truba. Have you ever heard of it?"

"Truba? Yes, I have. But why would you want to go there? Nobody lives there anymore. It's a ghost town."

"Ghost towns fascinate me," Jim said.

"Do they, now? Well, don't know what you could possibly find in Truba that would be fascinating, but it's about ten miles north of here." The clerk pointed toward a notch in a distant mountain. "Keep yourself lined up with that notch, and you can't miss it."

"Thanks," Jim said. "Where's the best place to get something to eat?"

"Try Vi's Pies," the clerk said. "She serves more'n pies, of course."

"Are her pies good?"

"She makes the best apple pie you'll ever put in your mouth."

Half an hour later, Jim took the last swallow of his coffee and examined the empty plates before him. The freight clerk was right. The pie was good.

"Would you like another piece of pie?" Vi asked, coming over to pick up the empty plates. "It's on the house," she added, smiling flirtatiously at him. She was young, copper-haired, and pretty.

"Thank you much," Jim said, leaving some money on the table. "But I honestly don't know where I would put it. It was a great meal, I thank you."

"I thank *you*," Vi replied. "And do come back, any time," she added. The inflection in her voice let Jim know that she wasn't necessarily talking about his coming back just to eat.

Outside, a train was approaching from the west, silhouetted against a sky smeared in colors—orange, red, and deep blue. Smoke from the engine billowed up in a rolling black cloud, and steam from the cylinders purpled in the fading light and drifted away. The headlamp, already lit, made a bright pinpoint of light against the front of the engine.

Night was falling, which was what Jim wanted. He was certain he would find Carmelita at Truba, and if he was going to rescue her, he believed he would have an easier time of it by using the cover of darkness.

Carmelita was being held in the bell tower of an old, abandoned church. The bell was no longer in place, though the bracket that once held it was. The bell tower had been converted into a room, which was barren except for the cot Carmelita was lying on, the table beside the cot, and one chair. There was not another piece of furnishing in the room, not even a carpet on the floor. The tower openings, which would normally have let the sound of the bell be heard, were now boarded over. The result was a room that was completely closed in. Carmelita was thankful that they allowed her a candle; otherwise she would be in the dark.

The town of Truba had died as the result of political corruption and big business payoffs. When the map of the proposed path of the railroad was released, it showed that it would pass right through the middle of the county. Enterprising citizens had bought land there; and built stores, saloons, a hotel, a church, and houses. Overnight, a town was born.

They named the town Truba, after Congressman Jerome Truba. Truba had taken money from the town's leading citizens in exchange for his promise to see to it that the railroad did indeed follow its proposed path.

But the leading citizens of Puxico, a small settlement ten miles south of Truba, had also paid Congressman Truba money for the same reason. The Puxico citizens were a little smarter than the Truba citizens. They knew how much

Truba had been paid, and they let it be known that they were willing to pay even more.

As a result of Puxico's participation, Congressman Truba got a law passed which gave the railroad free land along the right-of-way, provided that that right-of-way went where he wanted it to go. The railroad accepted Truba's offer, and rerouted their tracks ten miles south of their original plat.

When the railroad bypassed Truba, the town withered and died. Its bones now lay quiet and dark under a bright moon. The deserted buildings had broken windows, doors hanging crookedly on one hinge, and sagging roofs. The saloon was empty; the bar, mirror, and tables removed so that all that remained to suggest it was once a saloon was a faded, painted sign out front that read COLD BEER, 5 CENTS.

Jim had just passed a building with a sign identifying itself as the TRUBA DEVELOPMENT OFFICE; WE ARE BUILD-ING FOR THE FUTURE when he heard a voice. He stopped his horse and sat very quietly, listening. Looking around to locate the source of the voice, he finally determined that it was coming from a church. And, as he examined the church, he saw that this was the only building in town in which any light could be seen.

He moved into a position in the shadows just outside the church, and listened to the voices from within.

"Why did you feed her? You're just wasting food," one of the voices said.

"What do you mean, wasting food? She has to eat, doesn't she?"

"It doesn't really take much to keep a person alive. A piece of jerky is enough."

"I wouldn't even treat a dog that way."

"You know what's wrong with you, Foster? You are too softhearted."

"Yes, well, I didn't join the Texas Liberation Front to kill women."

Jim felt a sense of satisfaction. He had found Carmelita, and, clearly, she was still alive. Though, from the sound of the conversation, they weren't going to let her live much longer.

He had also, apparently, located the headquarters of the Texas Liberation Front.

Jim worked his way around to the rear of the building. Trying a window on the corner, he was pleased to find that it wasn't locked. He lifted it quietly, then slipped inside.

He found himself in what he assumed had once been the sanctuary. Moving quietly through the dark room, he opened another door. There, in the nave, he saw a lantern, tables, and chairs. There were four men sitting around one of the tables, engaged in conversation.

"What are you going to do with her, Malloy?"

The man who asked the question was sitting with his back to Jim.

"Foster, why are you so worried about the girl?" Malloy replied. "I thought your job was to win people over to our side."

"How can I do that when you do stupid things like taking innocent young women hostage? You didn't answer my question. What are you going to do with her?"

"I haven't made up my mind," Malloy said. "For now, she can stay up in the bell tower."

*The bell tower.* Now Jim knew where she was. The only problem would be getting to her, and getting her away from here.

Jim decided that the best way to approach the bell tower would be from outside, so he climbed back out of the window, but instead of dropping back down to the ground, he stood on the windowsill, reached up and grabbed the eaves, then, with some effort, managed to pull himself up onto the roof of the church.

Leaning forward, Jim half-scrambled, half-crawled up the steep pitch of the room until he was at the peak. Then he worked his way along the peak until he reached the bell tower, where he discovered that all four openings were boarded over with freshly nailed planks.

Jim used his knife to pry out several nails, doing them one at a time and removing them slowly so that they wouldn't make any noise. Finally, he had enough nails extracted to remove two of the boards. With the two boards removed, he was able to slip inside.

"Oh, thank God it is you!" Carmelita exclaimed. "When I heard someone removing the boards, I was praying that it would be you, or my brother."

"I'm going to get you out of here," Jim said.

Outside the door, they heard footsteps coming up the stairs.

"There is no time! Someone is coming!" Carmelita said.

Looking around the room, Jim saw no place to hide. His only chance was to go back out through the window, then hang on from outside. He did this, managing to get through just as the door opened.

"Señorita Gonzalez, it's me, Foster," a man said, coming inside. Before he closed the door, he turned and looked back through it to make certain no one had followed him. "I've come to get you out of here."

"Señor Foster, are you serious? You are going to help me escape?"

"Shh," Foster said. "My name isn't really Foster. I am Captain Bailey, of the Texas Rangers."

"Wait a minute, Bailey, I'm coming in," Jim said from outside the window.

"What?" Bailey gasped. He pulled his pistol and pointed it toward the window.

"No, Señor Bailey, he is here to help me!" Carmelita said quickly, reaching up to push the gun down.

"Come on in, real slow," Bailey ordered.

Complying with Bailey's order, Jim stepped carefully through the opening he had made in the window.

"Who are you?" Bailey asked. Bailey had not yet put his gun away.

"My name is Jim West."

"Are you the one who was following Malloy and his men?"

"Yes."

Bailey chuckled. "Well, you put quite a dint in his numbers, I must say."

Jim squinted as he studied Bailey. "We've met before, haven't we, Captain Bailey?"

"Have we? I don't recall."

"Sure you do," Jim said. "Think about it. A graveyard in Springfield, Illinois?"

"I'll be," Bailey said. "Yes, I do remember now. Captain James West. You are the one who prevented me from making the biggest mistake of my life. You have no idea how many times I've given thanks, since then, that you came along when you did. You could have killed me—or put me in prison for many years—but you didn't."

"You were following orders," Jim said. "We were on opposite sides, but we shared the misery of the war. It would have served no purpose to punish you for what was, in essence, a military mission."

"I have been true to my oath, Mr. West. I have never breathed a word about what almost happened there."

Suddenly the door was kicked open and Malloy and three of his men came rushing in. One of them was carrying a lantern, and all were carrying guns.

"Well, now, what have we here?" Malloy asked. "Foster, I had a hunch that you might come up here and try to set the señorita free. So I spread the word around among the boys. We've been keepin' an eye on you, and here you are."

"You've got it all wrong," Bailey said. He nodded toward Jim. "I heard someone up here. I came up to see what it was, and I discovered this man trying to break her out."

"Is that right, Captain Bailey of the Texas Rangers?" Malloy asked, sarcastically. He took Bailey's gun. "Put your hands up," he said.

Bailey did as he was ordered.

"What do you think, boys? We have arrived," Malloy said. "They've set the Texas Rangers on us."

The men with Malloy laughed.

"And who might you be?" Malloy asked Jim.

"I'm James T. West, agent for the United States Secret Service," Jim said.

"The United States Secret Service. You don't say. Billy!" Malloy called over his shoulder. "Billy, get in here."

The young man whom Jim had shot in the hip came hobbling into the room at Malloy's. The pain had obviously returned, for he was favoring his hip, and his face was ashen.

"Is this the man who shot you?"

"Yes, sir," Billy said. "And he's the one that kilt Deke and the others, too."

"You shouldn't be up and around, Billy," Jim said. "If you don't let that wound heal, it's going to go gangrenous on you."

"Shut up! I don't have to listen to you!" Billy said.

"I'm just trying to help."

"Your concern about Billy's welfare is touching," Malloy said. "Especially since you are the one who shot him. And the others. Mr. West, you have cost me some good men over the last few days."

"They couldn't have been all that good," Jim said. "Or they wouldn't have been working for you."

Malloy glared at Jim, then nodded to the others who were with him. "Tie them up," he said.

A few minutes later, Jim, Bailey, and Carmelita were all sitting on the floor. Back to back, they made sort of a living three-point star, as they were bound hand and feet and to each other. Malloy, who was the only one still in the room with them, came around to stand in front of Jim. In his hand was the small holdout pistol that Jim normally kept on a spring up his sleeve.

"I must say, Mr. West, you are a pretty clever fellow," he said. "Hiding a gun up your sleeve like that. Yes, sir, I'll just bet that little trick has gotten you out of all sorts of jams, hasn't it?"

"From time to time," Jim said.

"From time to time, yes, I'm sure it has. You know, Mr. West, it's too bad I can't talk you into joining up with the

Texas Liberation Front. We could use a smart fellow like you."

"You don't really believe you are going to be able to pull Texas out of the Union, do you?"

"Oh, yes, sir, I absolutely do believe it. And when Texas is an independent nation, I will be at the head of her army."

"The head of the army? Not the president?"

"We already have a president."

"That's interesting," Jim said. "You have no country and you have had no election . . . but you do have a president."

"We don't need an election. When our president takes office, he will have the support of everyone in Texas."

Bailey snorted. "You don't expect us to believe that, do you?"

"Oh no, Captain Bailey. I don't expect you to do anything but die," Malloy said.

"A firing squad, no doubt?" Jim asked.

"A firing squad? I must confess that the idea of a military firing squad does have a certain appeal about it. But firing squads will be for our enemies, after we have taken over. For now, I have devised a much more interesting way for the three of you to die. Several sticks of dynamite are placed at strategic points throughout the building. Just before we leave, I will light a slow-burning fuse. The fuse will burn for five minutes . . . then . . . BOOM! All the dynamite sticks will go off at the same time."

"Let the girl go back to her brother," Jim said. "There is nothing she can do to hurt you."

"Oh, I'm sure there isn't anything she can do to hurt me," Malloy said. "But that isn't the point, you see. The point is, I want to hurt her brother."

"Colonel, the fuses are set and ready to light," someone called.

"Is that so? Then we'll be leaving now," Malloy said. "Oh, and just in case you are able to get loose from the ropes, I think I should also tell you that the door is rigged. Once I close it, it cannot be opened again without setting off the charges. Good-bye, now."

Malloy closed the door, then they heard the clatter of his footfalls on the steps as he hurried downstairs. A moment later, they heard the drumming of hoofbeats as Malloy and his army rode out of town.

"I'm sorry, miss," Bailey said to Carmelita. "I should've tried to get you free before now, but I kept waiting for what I thought was the best chance."

"That's all right, señor," Carmelita replied. "I know that you are a good man, and I know that your heart was in the right place."

"Let's don't give up yet," Jim said. He raised his feet, then slammed them back to the floor. When he did, a knife blade popped out of the toe of his left boot.

"What are you doing?" Bailey asked.

"I'm getting us out of here," Jim replied. Working hard against the restraints, he finally managed to get the boot off. Then he started sliding the boot up his legs. When it got to his lap, he twisted around so that the boot fell on the floor alongside his waist. Using his hip, he managed to get the boot behind him. "Captain Bailey, scoot back against me as much as you can," Jim said. "We need to squeeze this boot between us to hold it steady."

Bailey did as Jim asked and, a moment later, the boot was in position for Jim to start working the ropes against the blade that was sticking out from the toe.

"Please hurry, señor," Carmelita said in a tight, barely controlled voice. "I can smell the smoke."

Carmelita was right. The smell of burning cordite was already strong in the little room.

"Got it!" Jim said when, at last, the ropes were cut. Freeing his hands and arms, he bent down to untie his legs, then he untied Bailey and Carmelita. A moment later, all three were free of the ropes.

"What now?" Bailey asked as he rubbed his wrists. "If Malloy really does have the door rigged, we can't go out that way."

"Do you think he does?"

Bailey nodded. ''He's evil enough to do something like that.''

''What about the window?'' Carmelita asked. ''Señor West, you came in that way.''

''And that's the way we'll leave,'' Jim said. Hurrying over to the window, he knocked out the remaining boards. ''I wonder how much time we have left?'' he asked.

''If he told us five minutes, then it would be just like him to give us no more than three minutes,'' Bailey suggested.

''If that's true, we have only a matter of seconds!'' Jim said.

''Ladies first,'' Bailey said, holding his hand out to help Carmelita climb through the window.

''Wait,'' Jim said

''Wait for what?'' Bailey asked.

Jim opened up the heel of one of his boots and pulled out a small pistol.

''What good is that going to do us now?''

Without answering him, Jim opened up the heel of his other boot, and pulled out something that looked like an arrowhead. He screwed the arrowhead into the end of the pistol, and pointed it through the window at an old general store that was just next door to the church. He fired, and as the arrowhead bridged the distance between the church and the general store, a line played out behind it. The arrowhead buried itself into the wall about six feet above the ground. Jim secured his end of the line to the empty bell bracket.

Taking a piece of the rope that had been used to bind them, he made a loop around the inclined line. ''This will keep you from injuring your hands,'' he told Carmelita. ''Hold onto each end of this rope, and slide down to the other side.''

Carmelita nodded, and Jim helped her up onto the windowsill. When she hesitated for a moment, he gave her a push.

''Ohhhh!'' she said as she slid down the line. Jim

147

watched her go all the way down, and was relieved to see that she made it safely.

"Now you," Jim said to Bailey.

Bailey didn't need a push. Grabbing a piece of the rope and looping it over the line, he was through the window in an instant. Jim climbed up onto the line and started down after him. Halfway down, the explosives in the church detonated. A blast of hot air hit Jim in the back, then flung him the rest of the way down. He slammed into the side of the old store building, then fell to the ground.

Smoke, flame, and pieces of wood flew up into the sky from the blast . . . then started raining back down.

"Under here!" Bailey shouted, as he rolled under the old store, which was elevated, since the building had been built on blocks.

Jim rolled under as well, and the three of them lay there until the last brick and board of the church came tumbling down.

"Are you all right?" Carmelita asked anxiously.

"I'm a little sore," Jim admitted, "but nothing is broken."

"Mr. West," Bailey said, "would the Secret Service object to you working with a Texas Ranger?"

"I don't think they would object at all," Jim replied.

"Then let's go get them. Oh . . . and it's good to be on the same side now," he added with a smile.

# 15

"You asked to see me, Mr. Lear?" Artemus asked. He was standing in the hallway just outside Cassias Lear's room in the Morning Star Hotel. The Cassias Lear Players had just closed a three-day engagement at the Waxahatchee Theater, performing before sellout crowds and providing, in the words of the local newspaper, "an exposition of acting so superior that one would have to attend a theater in New York to find a performance of equal caliber."

"Yes, Mr. Wilkes, won't you come in, please?" Lear invited.

When Artemus stepped into Lear's room, he noticed that Jason Noble and Malcolm Corey were already there. Artemus greeted them, and they returned the greeting.

"What is it?" Artemus asked, feigning nervousness. "Is anything wrong?"

"Wrong? No, nothing is wrong. Why would you think that?" Lear asked.

"It is in the nature of an actor to be nervous, I suppose," Artemus answered. "Anytime the director asks to see me, I worry."

"Well, you may put your worrying to ease, Mr. Wilkes," Lear said. "We are merely making plans for our Dallas engagement. I want it to be very, very special."

"Oh, yes indeed," Artemus said. "We should all endeavor to make every performance special."

"Ah, but our performance in Dallas should be even more special," Lear said, holding up his finger.

Artemus looked confused. "Why is the Dallas performance different from any other?"

"Mr. Lear, you mean you haven't told him?" Noble inquired.

"Told me what?"

"About our performing for the president," Corey said.

"The president? You mean, as in the president of the United States?"

"James Garfield, yes," Noble said.

"Oh, my! Well, I . . . I had no idea," Artemus said. "How exciting."

"I haven't told you before now because, as you and your niece are the newest members of our troupe, I did not want to make you nervous," Lear said.

"How can it be that we will perform for the president?"

"He is coming to Texas as a special guest of Governor Roberts," Lear explained. "And, as his visit coincides with our appearance in Dallas, we have been informed that he will attend one of our performances."

"Oh, how exiting. But it does make one nervous to contemplate performing in front of the president, doesn't it?"

"Don't get too nervous," Lear said. "For I shall want you to do a special act."

"A special act?"

"Yes. Do you remember the piece you did when you auditioned for me, the one about the man who comes home to find himself a cuckold?"

Noble chuckled. "A mustache on a mushmelon, I never saw before," he said, quoting from the piece.

"Yes," Artemus said. "Of course I remember. I have given that monologue many times."

"Then you would have no problems giving it on the

night we perform for the president?" Lear asked.

"No, I would have no problem with it. But won't we be doing *Hamlet*?"

"Yes."

"Then I don't understand. Mr. Lear, as you yourself pointed out, this is a comedic piece. It is hardly the piece one would give to prepare an audience for *Hamlet*."

"Surely you have learned by now, Mr. Wilkes, that there is ample room in the theater for both tragedy and comedy," Lear said, pointedly. "In fact, the line between pathos and comedy is very narrow. And on the night of our performance, we shall have uproarious laughter . . . followed by tears."

"We will give the audience something no one has ever seen before," Noble said. "Never has there been a performance such as the one the audience will see on that night."

"Oh, but there has been a performance of equal juxtaposition between comedy and tragedy, Mr. Noble," Lear said, holding up his finger. "I recall the night when a not very bright and not very good actor named Harry Hawk delivered the line, 'Don't know the manners of good society, eh? Well, I guess I know enough to turn you inside out, old gal . . . you sockdologizing old mantrap!'

"That rather moronic line brought uproarious laughter from the audience. Those words, and that laughter, were the last sounds Abraham Lincoln ever heard, for in a brilliant piece of theater, John Wilkes Booth used that laughter to mask the sound of the pistol shot that took Lincoln's life. Thus, the audience in Ford Theater enjoyed a supreme moment of comedy and pathos."

"Enjoyed?" Artemus asked. "What an odd way to refer to the murder of the president."

"Assassination is a political act, Mr. Wilkes. It is not murder. And even those who might have abhorred the act would have to admit that, on that night, John Wilkes Booth gave them brilliant theater."

"Yes, I suppose so," Artemus said.

"So, can I count on you to deliver your monologue on that night?" Lear asked.

"Yes, of course you can," Artemus said. "I would be very, very proud to do it."

A few moments after Artemus returned to his room, someone knocked on the door. Secreting a small palm pistol, Artemus opened the door. When he saw that it was Molly, he put the gun away.

"What did Lear want?" Molly asked.

Artemus looked up and down the hallway to make certain no one was close enough to hear, then he invited Molly in.

"Do you remember when I told you that Fitzhugh's dying words were, 'The president is in danger'?" Artemus asked.

"Yes."

"I now know what he was referring to. President Garfield is coming to Texas next week. He will be in the audience during our performance in Dallas."

"The president is coming to Texas?"

"Yes. And I believe an assassination attempt is going to be made then."

"Who is going to make the attempt? And why would anyone want to kill the president?"

"I don't know the answer to either question," Artemus said, "but I intend to find out."

## One Hundred and Fifty Miles Northwest of Waxahatchee

A hot, dry wind moved through the canyon, pushing before it a billowing puff of red dust. The cloud of dust lifted high and spread out wide, making it look as if there was blood on the sun.

Jim and Bailey had returned Carmelita safely to her brother, then picked up the trail of Malloy and two others. Bailey proved his value to Jim by pointing out the double-tie-bar shoe that was on Malloy's favorite horse.

"How do you know it's his horse?" Jim had asked.

"Because I put it there," Bailey explained. "I figured

there might come a day when I would have to track Malloy, so I decided to give his horse a special mark that would make it easier to do.''

Jim laughed. ''Sort of like belling the cat, eh?''

''In a manner of speaking,'' Bailey replied.

They had followed the double-tie-bar shoe into this canyon, and now Jim was squatting on the sunbaked ground, holding the reins of his horse and reading the sign.

''They are in here, all right,'' Jim said. ''The question is . . . where?''

At that moment, something caught Bailey's attention, and he twisted in his saddle to look up toward the high denuded wall of the red mesa that boxed in the canyon. He saw a flash of light—the sun's reflection off polished metal, perhaps.

''I think I know where,'' Baily said, pointing.

Jim stood and looked up to the top of the canyon wall. There was another flash, only this time it wasn't the sun—it was a tiny wink of fire. They heard the rifle's report an instant before the bullet hit a nearby rock, then whined as it ricocheted away. A little cloud of smoke drifted over the edge of the cliff.

''That's them, all right,'' Jim said. He pulled his rifle from its scabbard. Bailey climbed down from his horse with his own rifle in hand. Both men slapped their horses to get them out of danger, and they ran on down the canyon, the echo of their hoofbeats bouncing off the high, bluffing walls.

''There's only one way we're going to get them out of there,'' Bailey said.

''I know,'' Jim said. ''We're going to have to go after them.'' Jim pointed to a collection of boulders located near the base of the cliff. ''Captain Bailey, why don't you get into those rocks over there?''

''Where are you going?'' Bailey asked.

''Once you are in position to provide me with covering fire, I'm going to go up after them.''

Bailey looked at the rocks, then at the sheer climb Jim would have to make. He grinned. ''I suppose I should argue with you," he said, "but if you want to make the climb, go ahead. I'll be glad to do what I can from the rocks." He looked across the open space, then added, grimly, "If I can make it to the rocks, that is."

Bailey took a deep breath, then started running toward the rocks. Jim began firing as Bailey ran, but that didn't prevent Malloy and the others from shooting back. Jim saw puffs of dust and heard the bullets whining as they came near Bailey, but none of them hit him. The Texas Ranger finished his dash with a dive that covered the last five yards.

As soon as Bailey was in position, he started firing. Jim was glad to see that Bailey was an excellent shot, though it came as no surprise to him. He could well remember how close Bailey had come to hitting him as he had stood in the dark near Lincoln's tomb in the cemetery in Springfield that night so many years ago. They had been on opposing sides then. But now Bailey was an ally, and his bullets were coming close enough to Malloy and the two men with him to force them to keep their heads down. That gave Jim the opening he needed. He stood up and looked around, then saw a possible way up the side of the canyon wall.

Though the route he selected had looked passable from the ground, climbing it proved to be very difficult. Jim had been at it for roughly half an hour, but it didn't seem as if he had gained so much as an inch. However, when he looked back toward the ground, he could see that he was making progress, for by now he was dangerously high.

Jim clung to the side of the mountain and moved only when he had a secure handhold or foothold, tiny though it might be. Sweat poured into his eyes and he grew thirsty with his effort, but still he climbed.

All the while Jim was climbing, Bailey was keeping up a steady fire from below. Jim noticed, also, that Bailey was shooting first from one position, then maneuvering to shoot from a second position, then coming back to the first. In that way, he was carrying out the illusion that both of them were still down there, and Jim made a mental note to compliment him for his ingenuity when he got back.

If he got back.

On top of the mesa, Billy and Poke, the two men with Malloy, were beginning to get a little anxious.

"We should'a killed 'em back in Truba when we had the chance," Billy said.

"Yeah," Poke added. "We should'a shot 'em, instead of leavin' 'em there to be blown up."

"The question I have is, how did they get away?" Billy asked. "I heard the explosion. We all did."

"It doesn't matter how they got away," Malloy answered. "They did get away, and that's what's important. And if you hadn't got anxious and started shootin' before they were in range, we wouldn't have this problem now."

"I almost hit 'em," Billy said.

"Almost only counts in pitching horseshoes," Malloy growled. "We should be on the train to Dallas by now. Instead, we're stuck up here while our ammunition, food, and water is down on the canyon floor with our horses."

"You're our leader, Malloy. What now?" Poke asked.

"Take a look. See if you can see what they're doing."

"Are you crazy?" Poke replied. "I'm not going to stick my head over the edge. Their bullets are coming too close."

"Take a look," Malloy ordered.

Poke glared at him, then, staying on his stomach, scooted out to the edge of the mesa. He stuck his head over to look down toward where he had last seen them.

"See anything?" Malloy asked.

"No," Poke answered. He inched a little farther forward on his stomach, and as he did so, he dislodged several rocks, which tumbled over the edge then echoed loudly as they clattered and bounced all the way down to the canyon floor.

"How about now? Do you see them?"

"Still nothing," Poke started, then he saw a flash from within the rocks. An instant later, a bullet clipped his ear-lobe.

"Ow!" he said, putting his hand on his ear and backing

away from the edge of the mesa. When he pulled his hand away, a little piece of the flesh of his ear came with it.

"He shot my ear off!" Poke said, his voice strained with pain.

"No he didn't," Billy said. "He just got a piece of your earlobe."

"I guess that means they are still there," Malloy said, apparently unconcerned over Poke's injury.

"Listen, Malloy . . ."

"It's Colonel Malloy," Malloy corrected.

"Yeah, well, you might be a colonel, but right now the only army you got is me and Billy," Poke said. He was holding his handkerchief to his ear, and it was already turning red from the blood. "Billy is so stoved up with that bullet in his hip that he ain't worth two cents. And I just got half my ear blowed off. So, you can call yourself a colonel all you want. But the truth is, there's just the three of us left now, and we're in trouble."

"Do you have any suggestions?" Malloy asked.

"Yeah, I've got a suggestion. My suggestion is that we leave. Let's get out of here."

"How are we going to get to our horses?" Malloy asked. "They're down there in one of the draws."

"Forget about the horses. If we need horses, we'll steal them. The way I see it, if we stay around here any longer, they're goin' to figure out some way to come up here after us."

Malloy thought for a moment, then sighed. "All right," he said. "Billy, you up to hightailin' it out of here?"

"You two go on," Billy replied.

"We can't just leave you here, Billy, without food or water," Poke said.

"Go ahead, I'll be all right. If you leave, they'll follow you. That will give me a chance to get back down to the horses and get away."

"What if they come up here after you?" Malloy asked.

"Then I'll just have to take my chances," Billy answered.

•   •   •

Jim was still climbing. In front of him was nothing but the sheer rock face of the cliff. Behind him was thin air, and below him, a sheer drop of over three hundred feet to the rocky canyon floor. Sweat poured into his eyes as he climbed, but he put it out of his mind. He reached for a small slate outcropping, but as he put his weight on it, it failed. With a sickening sensation in his stomach, he felt himself falling.

Jim reached out to grab anything he could, and fortunately managed to get hold of a sturdy juniper tree. He slammed against the side of the cliff and felt the rocks scrape and tear at his flesh, but he was able to stop his fall. He held his position for several seconds, breathing deeply, then he started up again.

"Billy can't go," Malloy said.

"What does that matter? He said leave him, so let's leave him."

Malloy walked over to stand just above Billy. "Is your hip hurting you?"

"Yeah, it's hurting' somethin' fierce," Billy said.

"It won't hurt much longer," Malloy said. He raised his pistol, pointed it at Billy, and pulled the trigger. Billy fell back on the ground with a bullet hole in his forehead.

"Hey! What . . . what did you do that for?" Poke shouted in surprise and alarm. "He said he was willing to take his chances."

"Maybe. But I wasn't willing to take a chance on his taking a chance. I couldn't let him fall into enemy hands," Malloy said. "If he told anyone about what is going to happen in Dallas, it would set Texas liberation back five years."

"Texas liberation? Are you out of your mind, Malloy? Our army has been pretty much shot up. It don't exist no more. There is no Texas liberation, either. I don't know if there ever was."

"That's because you've never been able to see beyond the end of your own nose," Malloy said, chastising him. "You'll see. When we do what has to be done in Dallas, we'll have hundreds of people—thousands of people—following us.''

''Yeah, well, I'm worried about the two men who are following us right now.''

For Jim, the climbing began to get a little easier, then easier still, until finally he reached a ledge that showed signs of having been an ancient Indian trail at one time, possibly one that had existed until erosion had taken part of it away. He even found that he could walk upright, and shortly after that, he made it to the top.

''You think they're still down there?'' Jim heard someone ask.

''Where else could they be?'' Malloy replied. ''You want to look for them?''

''No, no, I got one ear shot off, that's enough.''

At that precise moment, Jim reached the top of his climb, and he raised his head to peek over the edge of the mesa. He saw Billy lying dead, a pool of blood surrounding his head. Malloy and Poke were no more than twenty-five yards away from his position, but they had their backs to him. That gave Jim the opening he was looking for. Unobserved, he stepped up onto the top of the ledge.

''You don't have to worry about where I am, boys,'' Jim said. ''I'm right over here.''

''What?'' Malloy said, spinning around. ''You must be some sort of a magician to get up here! How'd you do it?''

''You don't really expect me to tell you, do you? Magicians never give away their secrets. I'm afraid I'm going to have to put both of you under arrest. Drop your guns.''

Jim's gun was still holstered; Malloy and Poke had their guns in their hands, though neither of them had their guns raised into firing position.

''You don't really think we're just going to throw down our guns and come with you, do you?'' Malloy asked.

''Don't let 'im talk no more, Malloy,'' Poke said. ''The more he talks, the more chances he has to pull some trick on us. Let's just shoot 'im and be done with it.''

Malloy shrugged his shoulders and smiled at Jim. "Well, it seems like my army doesn't want to give up," he said. "And we do have our guns in our hands, while yours is still in its holster. So I guess we're just going to have to go for it."

Even as he was speaking, Malloy and Poke were bringing their guns up, thumbing back on the hammers. At almost that same moment, Jim threw a glass ball onto the ground in front of him. It burst with a flash of light and a billowing cloud of smoke. Behind the screen of smoke, Jim threw himself onto the ground and rolled to the left, as two bullets, fired by Malloy and Poke, punched harmlessly through the cloud.

"Where'd he go?" Poke yelled.

"There!" Malloy shouted, seeing Jim roll on the ground away from the smoke. Malloy swung his gun around to take aim for a second shot, but by this time Jim had his own gun out. He fired twice.

Two bullets were all it took.

Jim checked the pulses, determined that not only the two men he had shot, but all three men, were dead. Then he emptied their pockets.

"I was beginning to worry," Bailey said when Jim finished his climb back down to the canyon floor.

"I was beginning to worry as well," Jim replied. "Especially while I was climbing the wall." Jim reached into his shirt and pulled out an envelope.

"What's that?" Bailey asked.

"Train tickets to Dallas," Jim said. "I found them on Malloy. Do you have any idea why he would be going to Dallas?"

"No, I don't."

"I guess the only way to find out is to go there. You coming with me?"

Bailey shook his head. "I'd like to, but I need to report to my commander in Austin. With Malloy and most of his army dead, I've got a feeling the movement for Texas liberation is dead." He smiled. "Thanks to you," he added.

# 16

When the Cassias Lear Players stepped down from the train in Dallas, Artemus saw Jim's private car sitting on a side track. As he and Jim had been unable to communicate for the last several days, he was very happy to see the car there.

Shortly after Lear had them all check into a hotel, Artemus excused himself, saying that his niece wanted to have a look around.

"And as neither of us have ever been in Dallas before, I would rather she not walk alone," Artemus explained.

After leaving the hotel, Artemus and Molly made a walking tour of the city, going into half a dozen stores, strolling along Trinity River, and finally winding up at the train depot. Artemus had gone along a circuitous route in order to mislead anyone who might have been following them. When he was sure they weren't being observed, he and Molly stepped onto the private car.

The car was empty.

"Oh, your friend isn't here," Molly said.

"Not to worry, my dear," Artemus said. "I will send him a message that we are here, and while we are waiting, I shall fix dinner."

"How are you going to send a message?"

"This way," Artemus answered. Walking over to one of

the windows, he began pulling and raising shades until the five blinds were positioned in a precise pattern. "As you observed while we were walking, this car can be seen from practically anywhere downtown. Wherever Jim is, he will notice the position of the shades, and will realize not only that we are here, but that we are asking for a meeting with him."

"How ingenious," Molly said.

"Ingenuity is, after all, the mother of our profession," Artemus said. "Now, let me see what I can whip up for our dinner."

Jim arrived just as the bisque Artemus was preparing was finished.

"As usual, James, your timing is impeccable," Artemus said as he spooned the bisque into bowls.

"I got your message." Jim nodded toward the shades. "If I had known it meant come to dinner, I might have come sooner. Hello, Miss Porter."

"Hello, Mr. West."

"What are you doing in Dallas?" Artemus asked.

"It's a long story," Jim replied.

"Oh, I do hope it is entertaining."

As they ate, Jim described how he had come across a group of men attacking the coach of Carmelita Gonzales. He told of beating them off, of the subsequent attack on Gonzales's ranch, of Carmelita's capture, and of how he trailed them and subsequently rescued her.

"And here is something interesting," Jim added. "In the pockets of everyone who was connected with the Texas Liberation Front, I found hundreds of dollars in counterfeit money. The implication is obvious. They were involved in the distribution, if not the printing, of the money."

Jim also told how he had been helped by Captain Bailey of the Texas Rangers, mentioning that it was the same Bailey that he and Artemus had encountered in the cemetery in Springfield, Illinois sixteen years earlier. He ended his tale with an account of the final showdown in the canyon.

"When I went through Malloy's pockets, I found, in addition to more counterfeit money, several train tickets to Dallas," Jim concluded. "So here I am, looking for a connection."

"Perhaps I can make that connection for you," Artemus said. He told of finding the printing press, and of finding ink on the tympan that matched the color of money. "If the Texas Liberation Front was busy spreading the money, then I believe that the Cassias Lear Players have been printing it. But so far we have no proof. We haven't been able to find the plates."

"Nor the templates," Molly added.

"However, counterfeiting may be the least of our problems."

"What do you mean?"

Artemus told Jim about Fitzhugh, who had turned out to be a Texas Ranger names Charles Garrison. "He was murdered."

"Do you know who killed him?"

"No. He was still alive when I found him, and I asked, but he said it was too dark to see. His dying words were that he wanted me to get a message to Captain Bailey."

"Bailey? Then the Texas Rangers had already made the connection between the Texas Liberation Front and the Cassias Lear Players."

"Evidently so."

"What was the message?"

"Unfortunately, he died before he could give me the message. But I do know that it had something to do with the president."

"The president? As in, of the United States?"

"Yes, I'm sure of it. Especially since President Garfield is coming to Dallas later this week," Artemus said. "And, while he is here, he is scheduled to attend one of our performances."

"A president attending a theater performance. There is an unhappy coincidence."

"It's much more than a coincidence, I'm afraid," Artemus said. "I honestly believe someone is planning to assassinate him at the theater."

"Do you think it is Lear?" Jim asked.

"If Lear is not to be the actual assassin, I think he is at least a part of the plan," Artemus answered. Artemus told how Lear had suggested that the performance they would give on the night President Garfield was scheduled to attend would be a juxtaposition of comedy and tragedy. "Jim, if I didn't know better, I would say that Cassias Lear is none other than John Wilkes Booth."

"What?" Jim replied in surprise.

Artemus held up his hand. "Don't misunderstand me, I know he isn't Booth. But he has adopted Booth's mannerisms, he looks rather like Booth would probably look at this age, and, I think, in his own mind, that Lear actually believes that he *is* John Wilkes Booth."

"Your Mr. Lear sounds like a madman," Jim said.

"He is as mad as a hatter," Artemus agreed. "But, like many madmen, there is also an evil genius about him. I believe his idea is to disrupt Texas's economy with the distribution of counterfeit money, then bring on civil discord by the assassination of the president of the United States. Evidently, Lear feels that the people of Texas would then be ripe for the taking."

"With Lear himself assuming the position of president of the Republic of Texas, no doubt," Jim suggested. "Malloy said something about the presidency of the Republic of Texas already being decided."

"So that's the big picture. The question is, what do we do now?" Artemus asked.

"The first thing we do is stop President Garfield from coming to Dallas," Jim said. "Then we figure out some way to get Lear to show his hand."

"What about me?" Molly asked.

"You continue looking for any evidence that might directly connect Lear with counterfeiting," Jim said.

"Compared with the possibility of the assassination of a president, trying to find evidence to connect Lear with counterfeiting seems almost anticlimactic," Molly said.

"Not at all," Jim assured her. "If we are successful in preventing the assassination, connecting Lear and the others to counterfeiting may be the only way we have of putting them all away.''

*The White House, Washington, D.C.*

William Windom, the secretary of the treasury, sat in the outer office waiting for his visit to the president to be announced. The door to the president's office opened, and a rather smallish man with dark eyes and a full, dark beard and mustache exited. ''Remember my name, Mr. President,'' the man said, holding up his index finger. ''It is Guiteau. Charles J. Guiteau. I am to be your ambassador to France.''

''Mr. Guiteau, it will not be possible to give you the position you seek,'' President Garfield replied.

''But I have earned that position,'' Guiteau said. He pulled a newspaper clipping from his pocket. ''I wrote a letter to the editor advocating your election,'' he said.

''And I appreciate that, sir, I really do,'' President Garfield replied. ''But surely you can see that there aren't enough ambassadorships to go around for everyone who helped with the campaign.'' Garfield nodded at Walter, and Walter came over to take Guiteau by the arm.

''This way, sir. The president has other appointments.''

''If we had elected a Stalwart, I wouldn't be humiliated in such a way,'' Guiteau mumbled as he was escorted from the office.

President Garfield smiled at his secretary of the treasury. ''Bill,'' he said, ''come in, come in, I need a few calming minutes.''

''Are you still being besieged by office-seekers, Mr. President?'' Windom asked.

''They tell me that there are as many as one hundred thousand on the list, all looking for a position,'' Garfield replied. ''I am determined to be the chief executive of this nation, and not a clerk for the United States Senate.'' He looked around the presidential office and shook his head.

"My God, what is there in this place that a man should ever want to get into it?"

"The presidency of the United States is a position few men are qualified to hold," Windom replied. "You are one of those men."

"Thank you, Bill," Garfield said. "Now, what can I do for you?" He held out his hand. "And please don't tell me you are trying to find a position for someone."

"No, sir, I am not," Windom said. "Like you, I am being besieged with requests for positions in the Treasury Department. I have been as evenhanded as I can be, dividing the patronage between the Stalwarts and the Half-breeds, but that doesn't seem to satisfy either of them. They are an aggressive lot. However, that isn't why I am here."

"Oh? Why are you here?"

Windom took a telegram from his pocket. "I received a telegram an hour ago from two of my Secret Service agents. Mr. President, are you planning a trip to Texas?"

"Yes, I am, as a matter of fact," Garfield said. "I am leaving by train tomorrow." He smiled. "I must say that I am looking forward to it."

"You mustn't go."

"Oh? Why not?"

"The agents who sent me the telegram, James West and Artemus Gordon, believe that your life may be in danger. They have uncovered what they believe to be an assassination plot."

"What they *believe* to be an assassination plot?" Garfield responded. "But they aren't certain?"

"I don't know that anyone could be absolutely certain about such a thing," Windom said. "But they seem quite adamant about your not coming."

"How reliable are these agents?"

"They have been with the agency from its very beginning, Mr. President. I am told by my predecessors that they are absolutely dependable. If they recommend that you not go to Dallas, I would strongly suggest, sir, that you listen to them."

"Mr. Windom, you are aware of my . . . need . . . to get

away from Washington for a few days?'' Garfield waved his arm. ''You've seen what I'm having to put up with.''

''Yes, sir.''

''And you still recommend that I not go?''

Windom nodded. ''That is my recommendation, sir.''

Garfield pinched the bridge of his nose. ''Very well, Bill, I won't go. I have no desire to be a martyr. I'll telegraph the governor of Texas, sending him my regrets.''

Windom cleared his throat, and Garfield looked up at him.

''What is it? Something else?''

''Mr. President, agents West and Gordon think you should make no public announcement that you have changed your mind,'' Windom said. ''In fact, they suggest that, if you could find a way to absent yourself from Washington during that same time, it might be beneficial to their investigation.''

''I see. For some reason, they want whoever is planning this assassination to think I am still coming, is that it?''

''Yes, sir.''

''All right. I'll let them develop whatever little scheme they have going,'' Garfield said. ''As it so happens, I have also received an invitation to the twenty-fifth reunion of my college graduating class. I will let it be known that I am still going to Texas, but, at the last minute, I will take the cars to Massachusetts.'' He chuckled. ''It will be nice to see my old classmates at that. And the more interesting to see their reactions when I show up unexpectedly.''


*Dallas, Texas, Three Days Later*

The banner that was spread across Commerce Street read, THE CITIZENS OF DALLAS WELCOME GOVERNOR ORAN ROBERTS AND PRESIDENT JAMES GARFIELD TO OUR CITY!

In addition to the banner, the buildings were festooned with red, white, and blue bunting. The city band was drawn up at the depot, ready to break into ''Hail to the Chief'' the moment the president stepped from the train.

A speaker's stand had been built on the depot platform, and several chairs were set up in a fan-shape pattern in front of the stand. Here, Governor Roberts would welcome the president with a few remarks, and it was hoped that the president would respond with a few remarks of his own. A glistening carriage, drawn by a team of matching white horses, would then take the president and the governor to the Chandler Hotel. There, after a short period of rest, the president would join the governor for an evening at the theater.

The depot was crowded with people, all of whom wanted to see the man who occupied the highest office in the land. In an editorial, the Dallas Morning News stated:

We urge all to turn out to welcome the president. Not only is it our patriotic duty to make the president welcome, it is also the opportunity to show the rest of the nation that Texas not only belongs with its sister states in this Union, but is proud to be counted among that number. An enthusiastic turnout would go a long way toward dissuading those few misguided fools who are, once again, talking secession.

"Here it comes!" a young boy said, running back from the eastern end of the brick platform. "The train is comin'! I just seen it crossin' the Trinity River!"

There was nothing remarkable about the appearance of the train as it lumbered through the depot, and in fact the engineer looked out in some surprise at the size of the crowd that was gathered to meet them. The train rattled and squeaked to a halt, then, from the rear-most car, a man wearing a three-piece suit, high hat, and with a full beard stepped down.

"It's him!" someone shouted. "It's the president!"

The crowd swarmed in then, and the Dallas police department had to move in quickly to keep them from shoving in too close.

With a phalanx of policemen clearing the way for him,

the visitor was escorted by Governor Roberts to the speaker's platform, where the governor began to speak. The governor spoke for twenty minutes, quoting poets and scripture as he welcomed the president.

The honored guest was then invited to speak, and he stepped up to the platform.

"My friends, I am honored that so many of you have turned out to welcome me. Thank you."

There was a moment of silence as he stepped down, because the crowd, accustomed to lengthy political speeches, was caught by surprise. They had expected much more, but when they realized that he was finished, they applauded with as much enthusiasm as they would have had he spoken for an hour. Indeed, many laughed and commented on the fact that they had already been standing in the sun for a long time, and the brevity of his remarks was actually appreciated.

The governor escorted his honored guest over to the carriage, then they started through town, waving at the people who were gathered on either side of the street.

Agent Artemus Gordon was hot in the false beard he had affected to pass himself off as President Garfield. He was sweating profusely, and he was afraid that if he didn't get out of the sun soon, the adhesive that was holding his beard in place would loosen.

Only Jim and Molly knew that it was Artemus Gordon, and not President James Garfield, riding in the carriage with the governor.

"Mr. President, if you are too tired to attend the theater tonight, I will be glad to send your regrets," Governor Roberts said.

"No, no," Artemus replied. "I'm sure there will be many attending the theater to see their president. I won't disappoint them. Nor would I want to disappoint the actors."

At the hotel where the Cassias Lear Players were staying, Lear was very agitated.

"Where is your uncle?" he asked Molly for what was at least the fourth time this afternoon.

"I told you," Molly replied. "He got a nervous stomach and went to the apothecary for a physic."

"He will do his monologue tonight, won't he?" Lear asked. "It is absolutely imperative that he do the monologue."

"You needn't worry about that," Molly said. "He wouldn't miss this opportunity for anything."

"He had better be here for it," Lear said. "Everything depends upon it."

# 17

Like most of the other citizens of Dallas, Jim was at the depot when the train arrived. While the others clamored to see the man they thought was the president, Jim waited for the mail car to be unloaded. He walked over to see the mail dispatcher.

"My name is James West," he said. "Have you a special delivery package for me?"

The dispatcher looked through the incoming mail, then saw a small, brown package.

"As a matter of fact, I do, Mr. West," the dispatcher said. "Would you sign here, please?"

Jim signed for the package, then, sticking it inside his jacket pocket, hurried away from the depot while Governor Roberts was still giving his welcome speech.

When he reached the theater, Jim went up the back stairs to the box that had been designated as the presidential box. There he went to work, setting up a couple of mirrors and aligning the magic lantern projector. From his pocket, he took the special delivery package that he had picked up at the depot. When he opened the package, he saw a glass plate photograph of President Garfield. Jim put the glass slide into the magic lantern projector and adjusted the gaslight. A beam of light hit the mirrors, then converged just over a chair.

At first the image was blurry, but Jim moved one of the mirrors slightly, then adjusted the lense. The image came into focus. There, life-sized and in three dimensions, was the likeness of President Garfield. He was wearing the same three-piece suit that hundreds had already seen Artemus wearing, and he was sitting on a chair, leaning forward slightly, as if very attentive.

Jim went down into the theater and looked back up at the presidential box. The image of the president was strikingly real. Hurrying back up, he extinguished the gaslight in the projector, and the image disappeared. After that, he left the theater and went to the hotel to meet with Artemus and the governor.

"Let me get this straight," Governor Roberts said, clearly agitated. "You are telling me that the man I welcomed today, the man who rode through the streets of Dallas in an open carriage returning the waves of our good Texas citizens, was *not* the president of the United States?"

"That's what I'm telling you, sir," Jim said.

"Then, may I ask who in the Sam Hill it was?"

"I'm afraid it was me, Governor," Artemus said, now no longer in costume.

"Gentlemen, I want an explanation for this. And it had better be a good explanation, or so help me, I'll have both of you thrown in jail!"

Quickly, Jim and Artemus filled the governor in on their investigation of the Texas Liberation Front and the Cassias Lear Players.

"Yes, I know of the so-called Texas Liberation Front," Governor Roberts said. "They disgrace the name of Texas. That is why I have ordered the Texas Rangers to investigate that group, and to bring them to justice for any laws they have violated."

"Then we are working for the same cause, Governor," Jim said, without telling him that, for all intents and purposes, the Texas Liberation Front was already eliminated.

"I was sure we would be able to work together."

Governor Roberts, somewhat placated now, nodded. "All right," he said. "Tell me what you want me to do."

At the Baltimore and Ohio Railroad depot in Washington, D.C., President James Garfield alighted from his carriage and walked quickly into the waiting room. His appearance had been unannounced, and the several passengers who were there by chance were excited at the prospect of being in such close proximity with the president of the United States.

"Walter, make arrangements for a ticket to Boston, would you? I am going to talk to the people," Garfield said.

"Yes, Mr. President."

Unescorted, Garfield began greeting and shaking hands with the other passengers who were waiting. On a few occasions, a mother or a father would hold their child up toward him, and smiling, Garfield would reach out to touch the child on the cheek, in every case having something complimentary to say: "what a beautiful little girl," or "what a delightful smile," or "my, what a strong, handsome fellow you are."

The children, not quite understanding why there was so much commotion around this man, nevertheless warmed to his easy smile and winning way.

Charles Guiteau, who had appeared in the White House every day since his request to be ambassador to France, had learned of the president's travel plans when he happened to overhear a conversation. He hurried down to the depot, perhaps for one last effort to convince the president to give him the appointment he was seeking.

Half an hour before curtain call, Governor Roberts and Artemus, the latter disguised as President Garfield, entered the theater. There were already several people gathered out front waiting for the ticket office to open, and they cheered and applauded as the governor and Artemus passed by. Artemus smiled broadly and waved at them.

Once inside, Artemus said good-bye to the governor, then darted down the long corridor to the front of the theater, behind the stage. He was removing makeup and shedding clothes even as he was running, so that when he appeared just outside his dressing room a moment later, he was already dressed in the costume he would wear for his skit. He had worn that costume—bright blue pants and an orange and white striped shirt with a oversized, polka-dot, purple tie—under the three-piece suit. As it was July, he was very glad to be rid of the suit.

"Where have you been, Mr. Wilkes?" Lear asked.

"I'm sorry," Artemus mumbled. He rubbed his stomach. "I found it necessary to visit the . . . uh, necessary."

Lear opened his pocket watch and looked at it. "Well, no harm done. You are here now. You aren't too nervous to do your monologue, are you? I want to hear laughter tonight. It is very important that they laugh."

"I'll have them rolling in the aisles," Artemus promised.

The doors to the theater were opened and the audience came streaming in. They were in a festive mood. It was the first day of July. From now until the fourth of July, Dallas would celebrate with political speeches, band concerts, picnics, a rodeo, and finally, a huge fireworks display. The fact that the president of the United States was here to celebrate with them made the occasion all the more exciting.

When Jim led the governor up the side stairs to the private box, the magic lantern was already on. The governor stopped when he saw the three-dimensional image of President Garfield sitting in the chair.

"Amazing!" he said. He stuck his hand into the image and it glowed with light. "It is as if he is here in ghostly form. I am sure the audience will be absolutely fooled."

"I just hope it fools our would-be assassin," Jim said.

After the audience was seated, the governor, following the script Jim and Artemus had written for him, stepped out to the edge of the box.

"My friends, as the president is exhausted from his long

train trip, I won't prevail upon him to speak, but I did want us to give him a good, old-fashioned Texas welcome.''

The audience applauded, and the governor gestured toward the holographic image. Then, with another wave toward the audience, the governor sat down. A moment later, the governor got up and moved to the back of the box, out of the audience's sight. There, he removed his jacket and gave it to Jim. The governor then withdrew, and Jim took his chair. Because he was wearing Roberts's jacket, no one in the audience was the wiser for the change.

At that very moment in the prop room behind the stage, Molly Porter made a discovery. She had just about given up her search for the engraving plates, when she happened to notice the grillwork on the back of the throne. To the ordinary eye, it looked like nothing more than a decorative pattern of hatches and crosshatches. However, something about the pattern caught Molly's attention, so she moved over to the throne for a closer look. That was when she saw that the grill was actually a series of rectangles that were of the exact size and shape needed to hold engraving plates.

Putting her hand on the arm of the chair as she leaned closer to study the grillwork, she felt the top of the arm move. Curious, she opened it, and there, nestled in a hollowed-out place in the arm, were three sets of engraving plates, one set for a five dollar bill, one for a ten dollar bill, and one for a twenty dollar bill.

''Now, now, Miss Wilkes. You so know what they say about curiosity, don't you? How it killed the cat?''

Startled, Molly turned around to see both Noble and Corey standing there. Noble was holding a pistol.

''Is curiosity what killed Mr. Fitzhugh?'' Molly asked.

Noble laughed. ''In a manner of speaking, it was,'' he replied. ''And now, my dear, I am afraid that you are about to suffer the same fate.''

Artemus had not seen Molly before he went on stage, but he wasn't particularly worried about that fact. Jim had given her the task of trying to find the engraving plates, and he knew she would take every opportunity to look for them. What better time than now, when everyone's attention would be diverted by what was going on on the stage.

Artemus was a couple of minutes into his monologue, playing the naive bumpkin who was discovering clue after clue of his wife's infidelity. As he moved through each new discovery, the laughter of the audience grew louder and louder, building toward the crescendo of the last discovery.

Cassias Lear, with a derringer in his right hand, crept up the small, enclosed stairway that led to the box circle. The stairway was lighted by two hissing gas lanterns, and one of them cast his shadow grotesquely on the wall beside him.

In Washington, Charles Guiteau picked his way through the circle of admirers who were crowding around the president to shake his hand. They were so interested in the president that not one person noticed the pistol in Guiteau's hand.

Back in Dallas, there was another burst of laughter from the theater audience, this laughter so loud that, for a moment, Lear feared he may have missed his opportunity. But he knew that he had not. He had committed the monologue to memory, just so he would know where he stood relative to time.

Lear reached the top step. He stuck his head around the stairway and looked up and down the corridor, but saw no one. Checking the load in his pistol, he stepped up to the door of the presidential box.

It had been like this sixteen years earlier, when President Abraham Lincoln had been sitting in the chair on the left. Next to him was his wife, Mary, who was holding his hand. Beside Mary was Clara Harris, and next to her on the opposite end of the box was Major Rathbone, the man who was supposed to be guarding Lincoln. On that night, Rathbone had been the figure who was the farthest away from Lincoln.

And yet tonight, conditions were even easier for the assassin. There was nobody in the box with the president except the governor. He was virtually unguarded.

On stage, Artemus was coming to the part that Lear knew would elicit the loudest laughter.

"Well, I've been around this country
    maybe ten times or more.
But, a mustache on a mushmelon,
I never saw before.

As expected, a thunderous roar of laughter filled the theater.

Lear raised the pistol, cocked it, then pulled the trigger. There was a flash of light and a puff of smoke as the gun popped loudly.

In the waiting room of the Baltimore and Ohio Depot in Washington, D.C., Guiteau pointed his pistol at President Garfield's back and pulled the trigger. The gun boomed, women screamed, men shouted, and Garfield fell.

"I am a Stalwart, and now Arthur is president!" Guiteau yelled as several men nearby grabbed him and dragged him down.

In Dallas, Cassias Lear didn't wait to check the result of his pistol shot. Instead, he dashed through the box, put his hand on the rail, and vaulted over onto the stage below.

"Sic semper tyrannis!" he shouted.

The audience reacted in shock.

"Ladies and gentlemen!" Jim shouted from the box. "Stay in your seats and don't be alarmed. No one has been hurt!"

Lear, who had started across the stage, now glanced back toward the box. When he saw the president still sitting there, exactly as he had been a moment earlier, he gasped.

"What is this?" he shouted.

"Give it up, Lear!" Jim called. "You are under arrest!"

Lear had one bullet left in his pistol and he aimed at Jim

and pulled the trigger. The bullet whizzed by Jim's head and lodged into the wall behind him.

Lear ran off stage right and Jim vaulted over the railing to start after him. Lear ran out the rear stage door and into the alley behind, with Jim in hot pursuit.

As Jim chased Lear down the alley, he had a strong sense of déjà vu. On the night Lincoln was assassinated, he had chased John Wilkes Booth. But Booth, who had been on horseback, had managed to get away. Lear was on foot, and Jim vowed that there was no way he was going to get away.

Still puzzled as to why his bullet hadn't proven fatal to the president, Lear ran out of the end of the alley. One block ahead, he saw a freight train on the track. The train was just pulling out of Dallas, and slowly gathering speed. Lear realized that if could get to it before it was going too fast, he could swing up onto one of the cars. And, as the train was increasing speed with each passing second, it would be going too fast for his pursuer.

The train was going faster than he thought, already faster than he could run. He had only one chance, and that was to leap for it. He took a deep breath, then jumped. He grabbed the rung, realizing his mistake too late. The train pulled him off balance, then threw him in between the cars. Lear had only a second to know terror.

Jim saw Lear thrown in between the cars, then down to the track. He turned his head aside as the train passed over him.

Jim never heard a sound. If Lear screamed out, his scream was masked by the sound of the train. Car after car passed over what had been his body. The engineer, unaware of what had happened, continued to increase the speed so that, by the time the last car passed over all that remained of Cassias Lear, the train was doing over thirty miles per hour.

· ′ ·

When Jim got back to the theater, Artemus was in control of things. Jason Noble and Malcolm Corey were in handcuffs, and the Dallas Police had been summoned to take custody of them. The theater manager was there also, nervously trying to find out what was going on.

"To think that someone would try to assassinate the president in my theater," he said, almost literally wringing his hands. "Oh, this is awful, truly awful."

"What do we charge these two with?" one of the policemen asked.

"Possession of counterfeit money, until something better comes along," Artemus said. "And I'm sure something better will come along."

"Where's Molly?" Jim asked.

"That's what I'd like to know," Artemus replied. "I know she is somewhere in the theater, because she was going to take another look through all the properties. But I haven't seen her since before I went on stage." He looked at Noble and Corey. "I don't suppose you gentlemen can shed any light on her whereabouts, can you?"

"We haven't seen her," Noble said sullenly.

At that moment Jim saw a drop of something that appeared to be water fall on the floor. Unlike water, though, this wet spot began to smoke. Jim squatted down, put his finger to the wetness, then jerked it back rather quickly.

"Acid," Jim said, sucking on his finger to neutralize the burning. He looked up at the ceiling and saw where the acid had dripped through. "What's up there?"

"Up there? Nothing but a storage attic," the theater manager said.

"How do I get up there?"

"There is a ladder on the back wall."

Taking a candle with him, Jim climbed the ladder. When he stuck his head through the opening, he could see nothing but boxes, barrels, and piles of lumber.

"Molly? Molly, are you up here?" When he didn't get an answer, he started to climb back down. Then he heard it.

"Uhmmmmm."

It wasn't loud, but it was unmistakable. Jim climbed the

rest of the way into the attic and began walking around, the inefficient candle creating as many shadows as it did areas of light.

"Molly?"

"Uhmmmm."

He saw her then. She was lying on a table, her arms and legs spread out and tied. She was also gagged, which accounted for the muffled sounds he had heard.

Jim removed the gag.

"Get me out of here!" she gasped. "Look!"

Looking up, Jim saw a large spiked rack. One of the sandbag weights used to fly flats was resting on top of the rack. The rack was held up by a rope, but the rope was smoking profusely because a beaker had been positioned in such a way as to allow a steady drip, drip, drip of acid.

Jim started to untie Molly, but he felt the rope partially give way. He pulled away from her and looked up at the rack.

"What are you doing?" Molly asked. "Untie me!"

"There's no time!" Jim said.

"What?"

Jim looked around desperately for some solution to the problem. At that moment the acid completed its work and the rope parted. The heavy, spiked rack started down.

Molly screamed.

At the last moment, Jim's eyes had fallen on a steel bar. Grabbing it, he put it upright on the table beside Molly. As he hoped, the top part of the rack came in contact with the bar, and its drop was stopped. The sharp points of the spikes were less than an inch away from fatal penetration.

# EPILOGUE

Jim, Artemus, Molly, and the chief of the Dallas Police were in Jim's private railcar, celebrating the successful conclusion of the case.

"We've got enough to hang both of them, or at least put them away forever," the chief of police was telling them. "Noble swears that it was Corey who actually killed Ranger Garrison, while Corey swears that it was Noble." The chief laughed. "They don't seem to realize that it doesn't make any difference which one of them did the actual killing. The fact that they were both present when he was killed, and that they admit it, is all that is required."

The telegraph started clattering then, and the chief looked over at it in surprise. "You fellas have a telegraph set in the car? I mean, right here in the car?"

"It comes in handy from time to time," Jim said as he walked over to read the little strip of Teletype that began emerging from the machine.

"More brandy, Chief?" Artemus asked.

"Don't mind if I do," the chief said, holding out his glass.

Artemus poured more for the chief, then some for Molly. "Jim?" he asked. "How about you?"

Jim had a pained expression on his face. He didn't answer Artemus. Instead, he pinched the bridge of his nose and walked over to stare, quietly, out the window for a moment.

"What is it, Jim?" Artemus asked. "What was the telegram?"

"President Garfield," Jim said quietly. "He was shot today while waiting for a train to take him to his class reunion. He is not expected to survive."

Artemus sighed. "We failed him."

"You didn't fail him," Molly insisted. "You did everything you could to save him."

"No, Artie's right," Jim said. "We guessed wrong. We advised him to stay in Washington. It would've been better if we had let him come out here the way he had planned. He could have left the box with the governor. He would have been safe, that way."

The chief shook his head. "You don't know that," he said. "Under the circumstances, you made the right decision by keeping him out of Dallas. Who knows what would have happened to the president if he had come here? You were prepared to prevent an assassination attempt in the theater, but what if they had changed their plans? What if, during the open carriage ride from the railroad depot to the hotel, Lear or one of his men had been waiting with a rifle somewhere along the route, like in the window of the top floor of one of our buildings? He would've had a clear head shot as the president's carriage passed below him."

"Yes," Jim said. "I guess you're right."

"Of course I'm right," the chief insisted. "And while I am saddened that President Garfield was shot, I must confess to being thankful that it didn't happen in Dallas. I'm not sure the city could ever live anything like that down."

"When are they going to learn?" Artemus asked.

"What is that?" Molly asked.

"When are they going to learn to stop sending the highest elected official in our land out to the people without providing an adequate method of protecting him?"

# BASED ON THE CLASSIC TV SERIES

# THE WILD WILD WEST™ IS BACK!

## THE NIGHT OF THE DEATH TRAIN

Jim West is headed east on the fastest and finest locomotive ever built. Barreling at speeds up to 70 miles per hour, the train's out to break the speed record and get a young girl to New York in time for a life-saving operation. But a gang of international saboteurs who know the real reason for West's high-speed journey are out to stop the train dead in its tracks—and derail the whole country while they're at it...

___0-425-16449-7/$5.99

## *DON'T MISS THE FIRST ADVENTURE:*
___THE WILD WILD WEST: THE NOVEL 0-425-16372-5/$5.99

Prices slightly higher in Canada       ™ & © 1998 by CBS Inc.

Payable in U.S. funds only. No cash/COD accepted. Postage & handling: U.S./CAN. $2.75 for one book, $1.00 for each additional, not to exceed $6.75; Int'l $5.00 for one book, $1.00 each additional. We accept Visa, Amex, MC ($10.00 min.), checks ($15.00 fee for returned checks) and money orders.   Call 800-788-6262 or 201-933-9292, fax 201-896-8569; refer to ad #806

| | |
|---|---|
| **Penguin Putnam Inc.** | Bill my: ☐ Visa  ☐ MasterCard  ☐ Amex _____ (expires) |
| **P.O. Box 12289, Dept. B** | Card# _____ |
| **Newark, NJ 07101-5289** | Signature _____ |

Please allow 4-6 weeks for delivery.
Foreign and Canadian delivery 6-8 weeks.

### Bill to:
Name_____

Address_____City_____

State/ZIP_____

Daytime Phone #_____

### Ship to:
Name_____Book Total         $_____

Address_____Applicable Sales Tax $_____

City_____Postage & Handling $_____

State/ZIP_____Total Amount Due    $_____

**This offer subject to change without notice.**